"Tess." Tameka lowered her voice. "You're asking me to *cheat*."

"Listen," Tess said. "I know you couldn't care less about the Blue Mug." Her tone seemed to say no sane person *would* care. "But I feel like someone has to knock Kim Carson down a few notches. Preferably me. So I'm asking you to help. Is that too much to expect from your best friend?"

"Tess, *this* competition *is* important to me," Tameka said quietly. "You know I've been feeling like a loser ever since Marina gave me that award. So why can't *I* beat Kim? That way everyone's happy."

Tess looked a little embarrassed. "Listen, Meeki, you're my best friend and I love you. But when it comes to playing to win, you're not exactly a . . . tiger. You're more like a pussycat. Beating Kim is too important to mess up. And I really think I'm the best person for the job."

Tameka felt miserable. Who was she trying to kid? The new Tameka was still the same old "Best Assister" Tameka. "All right, I'll do it."

Best Friend
Face-off

Best Friend Face-off

by

Emily Costello

A SKYLARK BOOK

NEW YORK · TORONTO · LONDON · SYDNEY · AUCKLAND

RL 5, 008–012

BEST FRIEND FACE-OFF

A Bantam Skylark Book/September 1998

Skylark Books is a registered trademark of Bantam Books, a division of Bantam Doubleday Dell Publishing Group, Inc. Registered in U.S. Patent and Trademark Office and elsewhere.

ISBN 0-553-48647-0

Published simultaneously in the United States and Canada

Bantam Books are published by Bantam Books, a division of Bantam Doubleday Dell Publishing Group, Inc. Its trademark, consisting of the words "Bantam Books" and the portrayal of a rooster, is Registered in U.S. Patent and Trademark Office and in other countries. Marca Registrada. Bantam Books, 1540 Broadway, New York, New York 10036.

PRINTED IN THE UNITED STATES OF AMERICA

OPM   0   9   8   7   6   5   4   3   2   1

To Serena and Andrea Chestnut

FOCUS, TESS ADAMS TOLD HERSELF. SHE tried to beam the same thought to her best friend, Tameka Thomas.

Tess and Tameka were members of the Stars, an American Youth Soccer Organization team in Beachside, Michigan. The Stars were playing the last game of their spring season. The score was 0 to 0, with about two minutes remaining.

Tameka had the ball.

Tess watched as Tameka faked out one of the Asteroids' defenders. Tameka's ponytail of minibraids bounced as she streaked toward the goal. The Asteroid covering Tess dashed off, charging Tameka.

I'm open, Tess thought. She wanted to call out

to Tameka—but she was afraid of alerting the Asteroids that nobody was covering her.

Tess saw Tameka look up to read the field. She could almost hear Tameka's thoughts. She was thinking, *I've got to pass. But Yasmine's covered. . . .*

Tameka glanced toward Tess.

I'm open, Tess thought. *Send it to me.*

Then . . . *Bam!* Tameka whacked the ball toward Tess—a strong bull's-eye of a pass.

Tess galloped forward a few steps and slammed her right foot into the spinning ball. It whizzed toward the goal, moving so fast it blurred. The Asteroids' goalkeeper grabbed at the ball, but she was too late.

"Goal—Stars!" the ref hollered.

"Yes!" Tess half skipped, half ran over to Tameka and jumped on her back.

"Yippee!" Tameka spun in a circle, giving Tess a ride.

"Nice teamwork!" Marina Santana, the Stars' coach, called from the sidelines.

"That's the way to play!" yelled Mr. Thomas, who was Tameka's father and the Stars' assistant coach.

Play resumed. But the clock ticked down before the Asteroids got within thirty yards of the Stars' goal.

"That's the game!" the ref called.

Tess threw her arms in the air like a prize-fighter and did a victory dance.

"Happy?" Tameka asked.

"Yes. You know I love to win." But then Tess thought of something that made her frown. "Except now the season is over." She put her hand over her heart. "How will I survive?"

Tameka slung an arm around her friend's shoulders. "Aren't you and Yaz going to soccer camp this summer?"

Tess brightened. "Yes! A whole week of soccer and nothing but soccer. In other words—heaven."

Yasmine Madrigal—Yaz—joined them. "Great game, you guys."

"Thanks." Tess beamed.

"That goal was scorching," Yasmine added.

Tess nodded. "I *knew* exactly when the ball was coming to me. I think I was reading Tameka's thoughts."

"We have ESP!" Tameka said.

"I bet I could get you a spot on the Olympic team just because you're my best friend," Tess told

Tameka. "Our amazing psychic powers could be Team USA's secret weapon."

Tameka rolled her eyes. "Last I heard, you hadn't made the Olympic team."

"Not yet," Tess said. "But I will. In 2004. Or maybe 2008. Soccer camp is the next step in my plan."

"Hey, what about me?" Yasmine asked. "Aren't you going to get me a spot on the Olympic team?"

"Sure," Tess said. "You can be Tameka's back-up. You know, in case she dies or moves to Australia or something."

At Tosca's ice cream parlor after the game, the entire team gathered around one long table. Everyone was keyed up and talking at the same time. Tameka found herself trying to follow three conversations at once.

Marina clinked her spoon against her water glass and rose to her feet. She held up her hands to quiet everyone.

"Shhh," Tameka said. "Marina wants to say something."

Tess and Yasmine immediately stopped talking. So did the rest of the team.

"I want to thank all of you for a terrific season," Marina said. "As you know, this was our last game. Our AYSO league is closing down until fall. So this is our last time at Tosca's, too."

Everyone groaned. Tameka knew they'd all miss the soccer—and the sundaes!

"Should I give it to her now?" Tameka asked as she leaned toward Tess.

Tess nodded.

Tameka pulled a box from under her seat. The box was wrapped in silver star paper and decorated with a big silver ribbon. Tameka held the box toward Marina. "This is from all of us—the whole team."

Marina looked surprised as she reached for the box. "Thanks, you guys!"

"Open it," Nicole Philips-Smith called out.

Marina ripped the box open and pulled out a T-shirt. She held it up so that everyone could see the lettering across the front. It said WORLD'S BEST COACH. Marina made a "who, me?" face. Then she pulled the T-shirt on over the one she was already wearing.

"I love it!" she said.

Tameka saw Nicole poke Geena Di Gregorio.

Geena got up. Her right arm was in a cast, so she used her left hand to hold a small box out to Mr. Thomas, who was sitting next to Marina. "This is for the best *assistant* coach in the world," she said.

Tameka shot Tess a surprised look. She hadn't known the team was going to give her father a present.

Mr. Thomas took the small square box from Geena. He unwrapped it slowly and pulled out a heavy-looking glass ball.

"What is it?" Tameka asked.

"A soccer-ball paperweight," her father replied. "And a very nice one, I might add. Thank you, girls."

Marina stood up again. "I have something for each of you," she announced. She pulled a stack of certificates out of her bag and set them down on the table.

Tess and Tameka exchanged curious looks.

Marina turned her attention to Sarah Mere, a tall, clumsy girl who hadn't played soccer before that season. Marina picked up the first certificate. "Sarah, for you, the Best Two-Footed Dribbler Award!"

Sarah took the certificate. "I couldn't have done it without you, Tess."

Everyone laughed. Sarah had been a terrible dribbler at the beginning of the season. Tess had given her hundreds of tips—sometimes even when Sarah wasn't interested in hearing them.

Marina continued handing out certificates. "Fiona, I give you the Comeback Kid Award!"

That was funny too. Fiona Fagan had gotten in trouble with her parents earlier in the season. Her punishment: no soccer—until the Stars had helped Fiona convince her mother and father to let her back on the team.

"Tess, you're next," Marina announced. "I present to you the Most Likely to Reach Her Goals Award."

Tameka smiled as Tess stood up to get her certificate.

"Thanks," Tess muttered to Marina. She was blushing. After she sat down, she kept looking at the certificate and grinning. "I'm hanging this on my wall," she told Tameka proudly.

Tameka thought Marina couldn't have picked a nicer compliment for her best friend. Tess was very goal-oriented—in two ways. She loved to put the ball in the net. And she was a big believer in writing down her aspirations and striving to achieve them.

"For Yasmine, the Most Improved Attacker Award," Marina said.

"All right!" Yasmine exclaimed as she stood up.

Another great award, Tameka thought. Yaz had started the season wanting to learn how to make more goals. Now she was one of the best attackers on the team.

"Your turn, Tameka," Marina said. "I award you . . ."

Tameka felt a thrill of anticipation. She knew she'd been an important member of the Stars that season—scoring almost as many goals as Tess while making sure everyone got along. Now Marina was about to acknowledge her contribution to the team.

". . . the Best Assister Award," Marina said.

"Oh. Um, thanks." Tameka managed to flash Marina a smile as she collected her certificate.

Best assister?

Yasmine leaned toward Tameka. "That's the perfect award for you." Her dark eyes were

8

sparkling. "I bet you set up more goals this season than anyone else on the team."

I made *a lot of goals too,* Tameka thought. She had to force herself to return Yasmine's smile.

While Marina continued to hand out certificates, Tameka stared down at hers. She was feeling . . . not angry, exactly. More disappointed.

Best assister was just so . . . *yuck.* Tameka knew she was one of the best players on the team. So why had Marina given her such a boring award?

Tameka spaced out while Marina finished with the certificates. She was startled when everyone got up. One of the Tosca workers started clearing away their sundae dishes and water glasses. But nobody seemed in a hurry to leave. The girls lingered, saying a few last words to Marina or giving her a hug.

Tameka stayed in the background. She wasn't mad at Marina. But she didn't feel like hugging her either. *Best assister?*

When the group finally broke up, Tameka, Tess, and Yaz got into the Thomases' car. Mr. Thomas drove Yasmine home. Tess came over to Tameka's house. The girls poured glasses of iced tea and wandered out onto the porch.

Tess sat down on Tameka's front step and squinted up at the early June sun. "You've been quiet ever since Tosca's. Are you sad the season's over?"

"Yeah." Tameka sighed and sat down next to Tess. "I'm also upset about my award—Best Assister." She forced a laugh. "I mean, that's an insult."

"No, it isn't!"

Tameka moaned. "Okay, maybe not. But—I do more on the field than assist other people's plays."

"Marina was trying to say you're a good team player," Tess said. "And that's a big compliment. After all, soccer is a team sport."

"I know. I just wish my award had been different." *Something exciting like yours*, Tameka added to herself.

chapter 2

"WHO DID YOU GET?" TAMEKA DEMANDED.

Yasmine bit her lip as she scanned the paper she was holding. "Ms. James," she reported.

"I have Ms. James too!" Tameka held up her hand and Yasmine slapped her five.

It was Tuesday—the last day of classes at Beachside Middle School. Tameka, Tess, and Yasmine were standing on the grass outside the brick building, reading their class assignments for the following year.

"What about you?" Yasmine asked Tess. "Are you in our class?"

"Um . . . I guess not."

Tameka felt her heart drop into her stomach.

The seventh grade wouldn't be any fun if Tess wasn't in her class. "Who did you get?" she asked.

Tess's face was a weird mix of emotions. She looked disappointed—which Tameka could understand. But she also seemed pleased, and maybe a little embarrassed.

"I have Mr. Hollinsworth," Tess said quietly. She lowered her eyes and slipped her assignment into her backpack.

Tameka and Yasmine exchanged looks.

"But Hollinsworth only teaches the Great Brains," Tameka said. Officially Hollinsworth's class was known as the Gifted and Talented class. His students were the school's all-stars. They ran student government, played the leads in the school musicals, and won the top prizes in the science fair.

Tess shrugged. Her cheeks were turning bright pink. "Come on," she said. "Let's get out of here. We're free for three whole months!"

Tameka and Yasmine didn't move.

"Are you telling us you're going to be *gifted* next year?" Yasmine demanded.

"I guess," Tess said.

The girls were quiet for a moment.

Then Yasmine smiled uncertainly. "Well, at least we'll all still be in the same building."

"I'll be just down the hall," Tess said.

"It's not like you're moving to Australia or anything," Yasmine added.

"We can still eat lunch together," Tess said. "Nothing is going to change."

Tameka couldn't think of anything to say. Her friends were trying to pretend this was no big deal. But she knew—and they knew—that it was *huge*.

The Great Brains never hung out with the rest of the kids in school. They were always busy going on special field trips and, well, doing other smart-person stuff. Splitting atoms or something. Most of Hollinsworth's kids eventually went on to a special college-prep high school, where they studied things like Latin and calculus.

Tameka tried to feel happy for Tess. She knew Tess deserved to be in the Gifted class. Tess worked hard at school—she even did extra-credit projects if that was what it took to get straight As.

Bs had always been good enough for Tameka. But now she was starting to regret her laid-back attitude. She felt that Tess was moving into some goal-getting Gifted future—and leaving her behind.

★

That evening Yasmine and the rest of the Stars gathered at Lacey Essex's for a Beginning of Summer party.

Fiona and Lacey had set up tables and chairs in the Essexes' postage stamp–sized backyard. The table was covered with taco fixings, sodas, paper plates, cups, napkins, and ice.

Yasmine was sitting on a folding chair with her plate in her lap. "When do you leave for Ireland?" she asked Fiona.

Fiona licked sour cream off her thumb. "The day after tomorrow."

"Wow." Yasmine was still adjusting to the idea that it was *summer*. That meant no school and no Stars for three whole months. The no-school part sounded great to her. But no Stars? That part made Yasmine sad. She was going to miss her soccer friends big-time.

"What are you doing this summer?" Fiona asked.

"Going to soccer camp," Yasmine said.

"That day camp they're having at the rec center?" Geena asked.

"No—" Yaz started.

"We're going to Camp Aspire," Tess broke in. She shot Yaz an excited look. "It's held out near Manistee State Park. The camp is exclusively for kids interested in playing soccer in college or in the Olympics. Yaz and I are going together."

Yaz made a face. "Seven grueling days and nights of intensive instruction. Tess is actually looking forward to it. I just want to have fun. And improve my game, of course. I can't let Yago think he's better than me." Yago was Yasmine's twin brother.

Lacey wiggled her bushy eyebrows. "Are there going to be boys at this camp?"

"Nope, it's girls only."

"What fun is that?" Lacey asked.

"The fun comes from playing soccer," Tess told her. "It's a game with a ball? Remember that?"

Lacey picked a tomato cube off her taco and threw it at Tess.

Tess ducked, and the tomato landed in the grass.

"Where do the kids come from?" Fiona asked.

Tess straightened up and took a sip of her soda. "All over, I think. Do you remember, Yaz?"

Yaz's mouth was full, so she shook her head. The camp had sent her a big envelope full of information. Yaz had flipped through the colorful brochure, but she hadn't absorbed many details. The most important thing to her was that Tess would be there. She knew they'd have a blast together.

"This will be our first year," Tess added. "They won't let you in until you're at least twelve. I've been dreaming about Camp Aspire since I was six years old. That's when my first soccer coach told me about it. I've waited six *years* to be old enough to go."

"What's so special about this camp?" Nicole asked.

"Two of the players on the 1996 Olympic team were Camp Aspire campers," Tess explained. "And Bobbie Dorrow—the camp director—was one of Team USA's assistant coaches. If she thinks I'm good . . ."

Yasmine suddenly remembered something

she'd read. "A big part of camp is this tournament they call the Blue Mug," she said.

Tess nodded enthusiastically. "I'm planning to win it."

"With my help," Yasmine put in.

"Of course!" Tess said with a laugh.

Yasmine felt a buzz of excitement in her chest. Soccer camp was going to be the best part of her summer, hands down.

★

Tameka wandered over to the table of food. She refilled her cup of soda, feeling blue. *What am I going to do while Yaz and Tess are at camp?* she wondered.

Tess and Tameka had been best friends for years. But since Tameka had found out that Tess was going to be in Mr. Hollinsworth's class, she'd started to worry that their friendship was in trouble. Tess was going to meet new people next year. Smart people. Leaders. Kids who were more than *assisters*. Would Tess think those go-getter brainiacs were more interesting than her old friends?

I have to show Tess that I'm more than an assister

too, Tameka thought. She couldn't do anything to get into Mr. Hollinsworth's class. But she could make sure Marina gave her a better award next season. Then maybe Tess would think of her as an equal.

Tameka capped the soda bottle and walked back to her circle of friends. "Guess what?" she said as soon as there was a break in the conversation.

"What?" Yasmine asked.

"I've decided to go to soccer camp too."

Tess's mouth dropped open, but she still managed to look as if she were smiling. "That is so great!"

"Absolutely!" Yasmine said.

"But . . . why?" Tess asked. "Why do you want to come now?"

Tameka shrugged. "I just decided I don't want to waste that week lying around."

Tess gave her a doubtful look. "That doesn't sound like old laid-back Tameka."

"That's because it *isn't* old laid-back me," Tameka said. "You are looking at a new girl."

ON A WEDNESDAY AFTERNOON ABOUT A week later, Yasmine picked up the phone and punched in Tess's number. Tess answered on the third ring.

"Hey, Yaz! What's up?"

Yasmine held the phone against her shoulder and opened the refrigerator. "Nothing much. I spent the whole day packing for camp."

"The *whole* day?"

"Well, Mom took me to the mall to get some new stuff. The Sports Shack is having a big sale."

"I know. Tameka and I checked it out yesterday."

"Oh." Yasmine felt a prick of disappointment.

"I wish you guys had called me. We could have gone together."

"We would have," Tess said, "but we weren't planning on stopping there. We just popped in on our way back from the beach."

That didn't make Yasmine feel much better. Why hadn't Tess and Tameka invited her to the beach too? *Don't be a big baby,* Yasmine told herself. She didn't call Tess and Tameka every time she went to the mall or the beach. So why should she expect them to always call her?

"Anyway, I'm calling because my dad thinks we should start figuring out how we're going to get to camp," Yasmine said. "Saturday is only three days away."

"Tameka's mom is driving," Tess said. "Didn't Meeki call you?"

"No."

"Oh. Well, she must have forgotten," Tess said. "But Mrs. Thomas is definitely planning on driving you. So tell your folks not to worry."

"Thanks," Yasmine said. *And thanks for calling to let me know!* she added to herself.

Mrs. Thomas picked Yasmine up early the following Saturday morning. Tess and Tameka were already in the car. The backseat was littered with stuff they'd brought for the trip—tapes, books, magazines, snacks, pillows.

Tameka rolled down her window. She and Tess stuck their heads out.

"Hey, Yaz!"

"Are you ready to be transformed into a soccer-playing goddess?"

"You bet!" Yasmine smiled at her friends. It had been only a few days since she'd seen them, but somehow it felt like much longer.

Mrs. Thomas popped open the trunk. Yasmine helped her dad fit her suitcase in. Then she hugged her parents goodbye.

"Give us a call tonight," Mrs. Madrigal said.

"I will."

Yasmine's twin brother, Yago, was playing with a Frisbee in the front yard. "See you later, Spazz!" he yelled. "*Much* later."

"Goodbye!" Yasmine called. "And good riddance," she added under her breath. A week away from Yago . . . paradise!

Yasmine peeked into the backseat. Tess and Tameka had brought so much stuff, there wasn't any room for her. Yasmine hesitated. She wasn't thrilled with the idea of sitting in front. She didn't want to be stuck making nice-nice with Mrs. Thomas for three hours. Tameka's mom was pretty cool. But still.

I'm sure we'll switch places later, Yasmine told herself. She opened the front passenger door and slipped into the bucket seat.

"Would you be navigator?" Mrs. Thomas asked as she held out the directions.

"Sure," Yasmine said, taking the sheet of paper. "Let's see. We need to get on 196 heading north."

"No problem." Mrs. Thomas put the car in gear and pulled away from the curb.

"Let's have a tic-tac-toe championship," Tess said to Tameka. "The first one who wins twenty games is the winner!"

"You're on!"

"Can I play?" Yasmine asked.

Tess made a face. "Tic-tac-toe is a two-person game," she pointed out. "But you can play the winner."

"Okay."

Tess was crowned the tic-tac-toe champion somewhere around Grand Rapids.

Yaz turned around in her seat. "My turn!"

Tess groaned. "I'm sick of tic-tac-toe. Do you really want to play?"

"I guess not. But—would one of you switch seats with me?"

Tameka stretched and yawned. "You do it, Tess. I'm too tired." She pulled a pillow out of the mess and put her head down.

"Hey, that's my pillow!" Tess protested.

"We can share." Tameka pulled out part of the pillow, making room for Tess. Tess and Tameka cuddled up like kittens and closed their eyes.

Yasmine was fuming. Tess and Tameka had totally ignored her request! But she decided that begging to switch seats was beneath her. If they didn't want her company, fine. She played it cool instead, acting as if she were actually interested in discussing gardening with Mrs. Thomas.

Tess and Tameka catnapped for fifteen minutes. Then they started a card game that lasted a good 120 miles. They never once offered to switch seats.

★

Tameka dropped her suitcase and sleeping bag in front of a low table covered with stacks of folders. Two older girls wearing Camp Aspire T-shirts were seated behind the table.

This is it, Tameka thought, her stomach flip-flopping. *This is where the new Tameka is born.* She was excited and scared at the same time.

"Welcome to Camp Aspire!" one of the girls said. She had pale skin and a scattering of freckles across her nose. A messy mass of overgrown black curls framed her face. "My name is Molly and I'll be one of your counselors this week. Why don't you give me your last names and I'll tell you what cabin you're in?"

Tess stepped forward. "Adams," she said.

Molly trailed a finger down a list of names. "Tess?"

Tess nodded.

"Okay, you're in Barcelona. Bunk one." Molly gave Tess a big smile. "That means I'll be your counselor!"

"Barcelona?"

"Yeah." Molly smiled. "All the cabins are named after Summer Olympics sites. Atlanta, Sydney, Seoul—you get the idea."

"Yeah. Thanks."

"Helene will get you your welcome packet," Molly added.

Tess moved down so that she was standing in front of the other counselor, a girl who looked Asian.

Tameka moved forward. "Thomas," she said to Molly. Tameka waited nervously as Molly consulted her list. She hoped there wouldn't be any problem with her registration.

When Tameka's mother first called Camp Aspire, she'd discovered that Tess and Yaz's session was booked solid. In fact, so was the entire summer. The camp had put Tameka's name on a waiting list. A whole week had passed before Tameka had gotten the good news that someone had canceled at the last moment, making room for her. "Oh, you're in Barcelona, too," Molly said after what seemed like a long pause. "Also bunk one. Welcome to the cabin!"

"Thanks." Tameka scooted over next to Tess. "They put us together, just like we asked!"

The rooming arrangement cheered Tameka immensely. She took it as a sign that everything at camp was going to go the way she wanted. She could already see the Most Valuable Player award she was sure to get that fall. *Watch out, Camp Aspire,* she thought. *The new and improved Tameka is here and ready to play harder than ever before.*

★

Yasmine blinked in surprise. She couldn't believe what she was hearing. Tess and Tameka had asked to room together? How totally rude! Didn't they know she'd feel left out?

It's not a big deal, Yasmine told herself firmly. But she was bugged. If Tameka hadn't decided to come along at the last minute, Tess would be rooming with *her.*

"Madrigal," Yasmine said, trying to ignore the angry lump in her throat.

Molly checked her list. "Here you are. You're also in Barcelona. Bunk two. You'll be sharing a room with Letitia Jones."

Tess smiled at Yasmine. "I hope you don't mind that I asked them to put us all in the same cabin. I thought we'd have more fun that way."

"Oh sure—thanks." At least Tess and Tameka had made sure she didn't get stuck with an entire *cabin* full of strangers.

Molly pointed them in the direction of

Barcelona. Mrs. Thomas helped the girls haul their stuff across an open field—Molly called it the parade ground—and down a twisting path through the woods.

They found Barcelona in a small clearing surrounded by forest. The cabin was made of heavy logs that overlapped at the corners of the structure. A Spanish flag was painted on the door.

Yasmine went up a few concrete steps to the door, which creaked as she opened it onto a sitting room. The only furniture was a table with four folding chairs.

Mrs. Thomas came in behind her. "Pretty basic, huh?"

"I'll say."

"No TV?" Tameka said.

"You'll survive," Tess told her. "We're here to play soccer, anyway, not veg out."

A bathroom and three tiny bedrooms opened off the sitting room. One bedroom had just one bed, so it was obviously Molly's. The other two were furnished with bunk beds, two identical chests of drawers, a garbage can, and a mirror.

Tess and Tameka immediately dumped their stuff in bunk one.

Letitia Jones hadn't arrived yet, so Yasmine threw her suitcase and sleeping bag on the top bunk in the second bedroom.

"Well, I've got a long ride home," Mrs. Thomas was saying as Yasmine came back into the sitting room. "I'd better hit the road."

"I'll walk you to the car," Tameka offered.

"Me too," Tess said.

"I—I think I'll stay here and wait for my roommate," Yasmine said. "Thanks for the ride, Mrs. Thomas."

"You're welcome. Have a good week!"

Once the others were gone, Yasmine tried to shake off her crabby mood. She crawled up onto her bed and flopped on her back to try out the mattress. It was lumpy.

Seven days of camp, she thought as she stared at the nearby ceiling. *Seven days of tagging along after the world's greatest best friends. I wonder how many hours that is?* She was trying to figure out by multiplying 7 by 24 in her head when someone burst in.

Yasmine sat up and looked down at a pretty African American girl. The girl's hair was straight, and she wore it pulled back with a colorful scarf. She had on big silver hoop earrings and an orange-

and-pink sundress that looked terrific against her dark skin. Her long fingernails were painted a pink that matched her dress. She was dragging an oversized suitcase.

"Hi," Yasmine said uncertainly.

"Hey there! I'm Letitia Jones."

"Yasmine Madrigal. My friends mostly call me Yaz."

"Yaz? That's cool!" Letitia spun around, giving the room a two-second inspection. "I see you already took the top bunk."

"Oh. Well, we could switch halfway through the week if you want."

"Nah. I would have taken the top bunk if I had gotten here first. Listen, I'll be right back. I have to get the rest of my stuff from the parade ground."

"Want some help?"

"Absolutely!"

Yasmine dropped down out of the bunk, and the girls headed outside.

"Where are you from?" Letitia asked as she led the way down the path.

"Beachside, Michigan."

"I'm from Cincinnati," Letitia said. "That's in

Ohio. Last year my mother drove me out here. Eight hours in her little hatchback. We fought the whole way. This year I talked her into letting me take the bus alone."

"Wow."

"Forget 'wow.' The bus was the pits. The ride took *twelve* hours. I think we stopped at every nowhere town between here and—" Letitia broke off as they approached a small mound of bags and suitcases. "This is my stuff."

Yasmine picked up as many bags as she could carry. Letitia did the same and then turned back toward the cabin.

"So this is your second year?" Yasmine asked as they recrossed the parade ground.

Letitia nodded. "If you have any questions, just ask."

"Thanks." Yasmine was already beginning to feel more cheerful. Maybe it wasn't so awful that Tameka and Tess were ignoring her. She'd just concentrate on making some *new* friends. Like Letitia.

chapter 4

As soon as they were settled, Molly gave the girls in Barcelona a quick rundown of the camp rules. Letitia showed the others how to get to the mess hall, where they would eat breakfast, lunch, and dinner.

Tess was starving by the time she went through the lunch line with her cabinmates. She filled her tray with a tuna sandwich, salad, milk, and a little plate of peanut butter cookies. The girls took a table near the windows.

"Where did you get that T-shirt?" Tameka asked Letitia.

Letitia had changed out of her sundress. Now she was wearing shorts with a T-shirt that said

BEARS across the front. The shirt was soft and faded—it looked like one of Letitia's favorites.

"This is my team T-shirt from the Blue Mug last year," Letitia said proudly. "Each team gets a name and a color. The Bears are brown, the Wolves are gray, like that. The coaches made the names up years ago. Some people have been Bears two or three years in a row."

Yasmine bit into a plum. "Is the Blue Mug fun?"

"It's the best part of camp," Letitia said. "My team got incredibly tight last year. We stayed awake past lights out making up cheers and hanging out."

"Sounds great," Tameka said.

"So did the Bears win?" Tess asked.

"No." Letitia giggled. "We came in third. Out of three."

"Ouch!" Yasmine said.

Letitia nodded, looking amused. "We were the worst! But the Bears *always* lose. The coaches keep records of the winning teams going all the way back to the first Blue Mug in 1972. Bears have never won once. If you're a Bear, you almost have a responsibility to stink. It's tradition."

Tess gave Letitia a puzzled smile. She didn't

understand why Letitia was proud of a team that was so lame. She planned to make sure her Blue Mug team won—even if she *was* a Bear.

"I'm going to get some more cookies," Letitia said. "Do you guys want anything?"

Tess shook her head. "We probably shouldn't be stuffing ourselves so close to practice. I don't want to get a cramp this afternoon."

"Cramps aren't a big deal," Letitia said. "Usually you can get rid of them by breathing deeply. That gets more oxygen to your muscles."

No duh, Tess thought. "I know that," she said. "It's just that I don't want a cramp to slow me down."

"Tess probably wants to make the Elite group," Yasmine told Letitia.

"You bet I do," Tess said.

From reading the camp brochure, Tess knew the coaches would divide the campers into three groups, based on ability: Competitive, Advanced, and Elite. Later in the week, each group would split into teams, which would compete in their own division's Blue Mug. Tess's goal was to be on the team that won the Blue Mug in the Elite group. The best of the best.

"You can forget making the Elite group," Letitia told Tess. "Only about thirty girls in the whole camp make Elite."

Tess felt her temper flare. *Where does Letitia get off judging my ability?* she thought. *She's never even seen me play!*

"How do you know I won't be one of that thirty?" Tess asked.

"Because twelve-year-olds never make Elite," Letitia explained. "The best you can hope for is Advanced."

"I don't remember the brochure saying anything about age limits," Tess argued.

Letitia shrugged. "Well, that doesn't mean they don't exist."

Tess didn't say anything. She wasn't going to give up on Elite until one of the coaches told her she couldn't make it.

★

By the time Tameka and the others finished lunch, they had only five minutes to change into their workout clothes and hustle to the playing fields. Tess and Tameka decided to wear their new Camp Aspire T-shirts.

Tameka was starting to get nervous about playing for a new batch of coaches. What if they didn't think she was anything special? *That's not possible,* she told herself firmly. *I'm the same great player I was for the Stars—with an edge. This is the* new *Tameka we're talking about here!*

"Don't forget your numbers!" Letitia called from her room.

"Thanks," Tameka hollered back. She sat down on her bunk and searched through her welcome packet until she found a white plastic singlet bearing a bold, black number 99. She pulled it on over her T-shirt and tied it together at the sides.

"I feel like I'm in a marathon," she said. "Or a skiing competition."

Tess looked up from her own search. "It's very Olympic," she said, sounding pleased.

Tameka laughed when she saw that Tess had gotten the number 1. "Cool! I bet they assigned numbers as people signed up for camp. You must have been the very first."

Tess shrugged. "Maybe they gave it to me because I'm the best player here."

"Think again, Adams." Yasmine appeared in the doorway. She pointed to her own number—2.

Tess laughed. "Okay, maybe it *was* based on

35

registration. But I still think my number is lucky." She glanced at her watch. "Our first practice starts in exactly two minutes. We'd better cruise!"

"I have to go to the bathroom," Tameka announced.

"Hurry!"

Tameka was only in the bathroom for about a minute. But when she came out, she found Tess standing in front of the door, tapping her foot impatiently.

"Let's go!" Tess grabbed Tameka's hand and pulled her toward the door.

"Where are Yaz and Letitia?" Tameka asked as they left the cabin.

"They went ahead," Tess said. "Letitia had something to do."

"What?"

"Who cares? We're going to be late!"

Tameka's stomach turned over. *Practice is about to start,* she thought. *Time to show the new Tameka to the world!*

Tameka and Tess rushed down the path and joined a crowd of campers making their way across the parade ground. On the far side of the mess hall, there were six fields side by side. The closest one was surrounded by bleachers, and the campers were gathering there. A group of coaches stood talking to each other.

Tameka slipped into a bleacher. Tess sat next to her.

"Welcome to Camp Aspire! Let's simmer down, please!"

Tameka saw that one of the coaches was holding a portable microphone. She had glasses, short gray hair, and a Camp Aspire sweatshirt. After the crowd of campers quieted down, the woman introduced herself as Bobbie. She said she was the head coach and camp director.

Tess nudged Tameka. "That's *her*," she whispered excitedly. "The woman I told you about, the one who was an Olympic coach."

"Cool," Tameka whispered back. But this information only made her more nervous.

"We need all the twelve-, thirteen-, and fourteen-year-olds to meet Craig on field one," Bobbie said after making a few general announcements.

"That's us!" Tess was already on her feet.

Tameka and Tess hurried over to field one, which was farthest from the mess hall. They were the first to arrive.

A man who was about the same age as Tameka's dad jogged up to them. He was bald except for a tuft of sandy-colored hair on either side of his head. "Hi! I'm Craig."

"Tess."

"Tameka."

"Nice to meet you. Grab a ball and do some juggling. Might as well start warming up while we wait for the others to arrive."

Tess and Tameka each got a ball. Tameka juggled hers on her thighs, concentrating on keeping control. The familiar exercise helped calm her nerves.

A few minutes later Tameka saw Letitia and Yasmine walk up. They were whispering and giggling about something. Tameka wanted to say hello, but they were so deep in conversation, she didn't want to interrupt.

Tameka wondered what Yaz and Letitia were laughing about. How could they be so chummy when they'd only known each other for a few hours?

After everyone arrived, Craig asked them to form a circle. He helped the girls stretch out from their toes all the way up to their necks. Then they did a series of more active exercises: passing the ball around their legs in figure eights, circling the ball around their waists, doing dribble sprints and jumping cones.

"Now we're going to start a shooting drill," Craig announced. "Choose a partner. Each pair will need two cones and one ball. Set the cones between you, about eight feet apart. Take turns shooting the ball to each other through the cones. Go!"

Tameka gestured to Tess that they should be partners. They quickly collected their equipment and staked out a position on the field. Tameka saw that Yasmine and Letitia were working together.

Tess set up the cones, and they began to shoot. Tameka felt warmed up and ready to go. She slowly got into the rhythm of shooting, stopping or running after Tess's shot, then shooting again.

After they'd been doing the drill for a while, Tess raised her eyebrows at Tameka. "We're being watched," she whispered.

Tameka glanced up and saw a cluster of coaches walking along the sidelines. They were carrying pens and clipboards. As they observed the drill, they made notes.

Tess seemed unconcerned. She retrieved her ball and made a beautiful shot.

This is the moment you've been waiting for, Tameka reminded herself. She concentrated on shutting out everything else that was happening on the field. She even stopped paying attention to what Tess was doing.

Tameka made shot after shot. Sometimes she whacked the ball through the grass. Other times she popped it up high. She tried to shoot with each foot instead of relying on her strong right leg.

"Nice intensity, number ninety-nine!"

Craig was giving Tameka a thumbs-up from the sidelines. *I hope the other coaches were impressed too,* she thought.

Next Craig ran them through a dribbling drill. Once in a while the group of coaches would wander back, still scribbling away on their clipboards. Tameka did her best to focus on the ball and keep her energy up. She was determined to play hard and end up in a good group.

Craig moved on to yet another drill. Tameka was dripping with sweat and her legs were burning. *Keep going,* she encouraged herself. She didn't want any of the coaches writing down that number 99 was lazy.

Finally Craig clapped his hands. "Okay, girls, gather around."

Tameka chose a spot near Yasmine and Letitia. She wiped the sweat off her forehead as she waited to hear what Craig would say.

"Good work, everyone," he started. "Excuse me if I haven't caught all your names yet. Number ninety-nine, you are . . ."

"Tameka Thomas."

"Beautiful work out there, Tameka. I love your focus. Keep it up." Craig went on to give a comment to another player.

Tameka felt about ten feet tall. She knew she had played well that afternoon, aggressively putting the ball exactly where she wanted. She hadn't been her usual relaxed self. But having the coach single her out? She'd never expected that. What a rush!

"Tomorrow we're going to break you up into sections based on ability," Craig said a moment later. "Before practice tomorrow morning, get your section assignments in the mess hall. Good luck!"

When Craig dismissed them, Tameka immediately trotted over to the water cooler. Most of the other girls followed her.

Tameka was so thirsty, she felt as though her throat were swollen shut. She filled a paper cup with cool water and then stepped out of the way as Tess filled her own cup.

As Tameka chugged down her water, she reviewed the afternoon's practice. She had taken a couple of big gulps before she realized something was wrong and spat out the water.

"Gross!" she exclaimed. "What's wrong with this?"

Tess made an I'm-going-to-throw-up face. "It's salt water!"

WHEN TESS GOT BACK TO THE CABIN, she headed straight for the bathroom. She turned on the cold water, filled her cupped hands, and slurped the water into her mouth.

After a minute she stepped aside to give Tameka a turn.

Yasmine was watching—and laughing—from the bathroom door. Letitia came in to watch too. "Thirsty, Tess?" she asked innocently.

"Did you have something to do with that salted water?" Tess asked.

Letitia nodded proudly. "Pretty funny, huh?"

Tess forced a smile. "Well . . . it was definitely a surprise."

Tameka turned away from the sink. "I was wondering why you guys didn't line up for a drink!"

"I've been planning this for weeks," Letitia said with satisfaction. "And let me tell you, pulling it off wasn't easy! I had to sneak into the equipment room while Bobbie was giving her welcome speech."

Tess nodded, ready to change the subject. "Oh. So what group—"

"But it was worth the trouble!" Letitia rushed on. "I wish you could have seen the looks on your faces after you chugged down some of that nasty stuff. Talk about funny!"

Yasmine laughed. "Tameka drank about half a glass!"

"I was thirsty," Tameka said. "And now I'm even more thirsty!"

Letitia hooted. "I guess I should have told you guys—since you're my cabinmates and everything. But I thought Craig might get suspicious if we all hung back."

"That's okay," Tess said. "Anyway, I was wondering—"

"Did you know what she was up to?" Tameka asked Yasmine.

Yasmine nodded. "I helped! I was Letitia's lookout while she was in the equipment room."

"So *that's* what you guys were whispering about!" Tameka said.

"Uh-huh." Letitia looked pleased.

"Anyway!" Tess said loudly. "I was thinking about which group we'll end up in."

The other girls finally turned their attention to her. They looked as if they didn't know what she was talking about.

"Group?" Letitia asked.

"Yeah," Tess said. "I was checking out the other players. I don't think *thirty* of them were better than—"

Letitia made an impatient movement with her hand. "I already told you. Twelve-year-olds don't make Elite."

Tess stared at Letitia. She didn't like to be told what she could and couldn't do. "Well, maybe I can change that," she said.

Letitia rolled her eyes. "Why don't you lighten up?"

Tess shrugged. She had no intention of lightening up. She saw camp as a chance to get *serious*. But she didn't see any point in telling Letitia that. She'd probably turn it into a joke.

"I'm going to go get cleaned up for dinner," she said instead.

★

Tameka stood next to Tess in the dinner line. "So, what do you think of Letitia?" she asked.

"She's okay." Tess helped herself to a tray. "But I don't think we'll be best buddies. She's not my type."

Tess moved down, and Tameka got a tray of her own. She plucked a napkin, spoon, fork, and knife out of a plastic bin.

Letitia and Yasmine appeared on Tameka's other side.

"What's for dinner?" Letitia demanded. "Ooh— butterscotch pudding. That's my favorite. Grab me *two* of those!"

Tess leaned forward so that she could see Letitia. "You're going to eat *pudding* for dinner?"

"Not *just* pudding."

"That's good," Tess said.

"I might have some of those lemon cookies too," Letitia said.

Yasmine and Tameka cracked up. Tameka decided she didn't care what Tess thought. She thought Letitia was fun.

★

Just after dark that evening, the entire camp gathered for a welcome bonfire on the beach. The counselors were holding marshmallows over the flames, then using them to make yummy s'mores.

Lots of the campers knew each other from previous summers. Everyone wandered around, chatting and catching up with old friends. Tess hung back as Letitia introduced Yaz and Tameka to her cabinmates from the summer before.

She looked up at the sky. The moon looked enormous, and the stars were twinkling. *It's a magical night*, Tess thought. *And the beginning of an important week.* She stared into the dancing fire, hardly believing she was finally at Camp Aspire.

More than anything in the world, Tess wanted to catch Bobbie's eye that week. She knew Bobbie could help her get on the Olympic team. Tess realized that some of her friends thought she was joking about going to the Olympics someday. She even guessed that they laughed at her dreams behind her back. But Tess didn't care. She knew she was good enough to make Team USA. Camp Aspire was the place she'd prove it.

"Check it out," Yasmine said, nudging Tess out of her daydream. "Molly is going to sing."

Molly had stepped in front of the bonfire. She was strumming a guitar. Tess immediately recognized the tune. It was from that silly song that started "Hello Muddah, hello Faddah, here I am at Camp Granada."

"Hey, everyone, welcome—or welcome back—to Camp Aspire," Molly said warmly. "What do you say we start the week off right with a rousing chorus of our camp song?"

The campers cheered and clapped. Tess struggled to hear the words as they sang.

"Here we are at Camp Aspire,
Gathered round a great big fire,
In a few days we'll start vying,
For a mug, royal blue and oh so inviting."

Tameka made a face. "Corny!"

But Tess liked the song. In fact she liked everything about Camp Aspire. She planned to learn as much as she could in the next week. And in the process, she'd show the coaches they had a future Olympic star in their midst.

★

When Tess woke up the next morning, sunlight was streaming through the window. She sat up in her bunk, wondering what time it was. Apparently not that late, since Tameka was still snoozing away in the lower bunk.

Tess rubbed her eyes and then pulled her alarm clock toward her: 8:42. *Huh?* Tess thought. *It can't be 8:42. I set the alarm for 7:30.*

She climbed off the bunk and padded out of the room in her bare feet. She peeked into Yasmine and Letitia's room. Both beds were empty and unmade. Tess looked in the bathroom. Nobody was there.

Moving faster now, Tess went back into her own bedroom. She picked up her watch from her dressing table. It read 8:45.

"Tameka, wake up!" Tess said loudly. "Practice starts in fifteen minutes."

"Mmmm . . ." Tameka rolled over to face the wall.

Tess gave her friend an impatient shake. "Meeki, practice is about to start!"

Tameka rolled back over and opened her eyes. "What happened to the alarm?"

Tess groaned. She was already pulling off her pajamas. "I set it, but it didn't go off."

"Why not?" Tameka sat up.

Tess pulled a clean T-shirt over her head. "I don't know. Maybe it's broken."

Tameka shook her head. She stood up, grabbed her bath kit, and headed toward the bathroom.

"Don't be long!" Tess called after her.

"I'm just going to brush my teeth!"

Tess pulled on her shorts and socks and then sat down to brush her hair. She wore it long, almost down to her waist. She gritted her teeth as she brushed it out. She'd gone to sleep with her hair damp. Big mistake. During the night it had clumped up in knots.

By the time Tess had managed to create a halfway decent ponytail, Tameka was out of the bathroom and dressed.

Tess's clock read 8:49. Not bad. If they ran across the parade ground, they would have enough time to get to the mess hall, find out what group they were in, and grab a muffin or something for breakfast.

Tameka slung her cleats over her shoulder and picked up the clock. "It's not broken. Someone must have turned it off."

Tess plopped down on her bed and picked up one of her sneakers. "I only know one person who'd—" Tess slipped her foot into a shoe and felt something ooze. She pulled her foot out and saw that her white tube sock was covered with something purple. "What the—"

"What *is* that?" Tameka asked.

Tess sniffed at her sock. "Jelly. Grape, I think." She peered into her other shoe. Sure enough, it was full of purple clumps too.

"What am I supposed to do now?" Tess demanded.

Tameka seemed too sleepy to get upset. "Take off your socks and deal with them later. Put on a clean pair, and wear your cleats until we can rinse out your sneakers."

"Fine!" Tess shouted. She opened her dresser drawer, grabbed a clean pair of socks, and then slammed the drawer. Somehow, making noise helped her calm down.

They finally got out of the cabin and arrived at the mess hall just as most of the campers were wandering out.

"Let's get our assignments," Tess suggested. "That's more important than breakfast right now."

Tameka nodded. They quickly located the computer printouts that were taped to the outside wall.

Tess found the list of Elites. The names were arranged in alphabetical order. The list skipped from *Abrams, Rachel* to *Austin, Karen*. No Adams.

I've got to be here, Tess thought stubbornly. She kept scanning—right into the Bs.

"I'm in the Advanced group!" Tameka announced. "Look, here you are too."

"Are you sure?" Tess moved over to look at the list Tameka was consulting.

"Hey! You guys missed breakfast!"

"What's the matter? Did you oversleep?"

Tess turned around in time to see Yasmine and Letitia come out of the mess hall. They were cracking up.

"We did oversleep—thanks to you," Tess snapped.

Letitia stopped smiling. "You're mad? About a little jelly in your shoes?" She looked shocked.

"You bet I'm mad! Listen, spend your time playing stupid jokes if that makes you happy, but leave *me* alone!"

"No problem," Letitia whispered.

★

"I brought you an apple," Yasmine told Tameka on the way over to the fields. "I didn't want you to go hungry."

"Thanks," Tameka said.

"I got one for Tess too," Yasmine added. "I'm going to try to catch up with her."

"Okay," Tameka said as Yasmine broke into a jog. Tess was about a hundred yards ahead of the other girls. She had stormed off after yelling at Letitia.

Tameka fell into step with Letitia. "You okay?"

"I guess. Is she *that* mad about a harmless practical joke?"

Tameka sighed. "Maybe. She's really serious when it comes to soccer. But I think she's also disappointed she didn't make the Elite group. She was probably taking that out on you."

Letitia made an irritated sound. "But I *told* her twelve-year-olds aren't allowed to be Elites! Bobbie thinks it's dangerous for kids your age to play with the eighteen-year-olds."

"I guess Tess thought they'd make an exception for her."

"Give me a break!"

"Well, that's Tess. So what group are you in?"

"Advanced. So's Yaz."

"Great! We're all together."

Letitia made a face. "Yeah, great. This way it will be easier for Tess to kill me."

Tameka laughed. "She's not that bad. You'll see."

BOBBIE WAS WAITING FOR THE ADVANCED players on field three. Craig was with her. So was another coach Tameka hadn't met yet. Her name tag said LIZ.

Time to focus, Tameka reminded herself. She tried to put worries about Tess and Letitia's fight out of her mind and concentrate on playing aggressively.

"Okay, girls," Bobbie called. "I'd like to start with an announcement before you get warmed up. As most of you know, we'll spend the next three days on drills and scrimmages. You'll have plenty of opportunity to improve your skills. Then, for the last three days, our schedule will change."

"The Blue Mug!" shouted a girl wearing a Major League Soccer T-shirt.

"That's right," Bobbie said with a grin. "For those of you who don't know, the Blue Mug is a tournament of drills and scrimmages. For the tournament, the Advanced group will be divided into three teams. Each team will have a captain. And at the end of the week, one of the teams will have their blue mugs!"

Bobbie gave the girl a big smile and then went on. "I'm telling you all this now because I want you to think about who would be a good captain. You'll have an opportunity to nominate people at dinner tomorrow. The coaches will make the final choices based on leadership and playing ability. Okay—let's get started."

★

After doing a few hip stretches during warm-up, Tess found herself relaxing. She regretted losing her cool with Letitia. Oh well. Maybe she'd apologize later.

"Okay, girls, pair up!" Bobbie called. "Then get into two lines facing your partners."

Tess and Tameka got in line across from each other. So did Letitia and Yasmine.

Bobbie walked up to the end of one line. "I want everyone in this line to shift down one," she called.

Tess took a step to her left.

"The person you are now facing is your partner for today," Bobbie announced. "Tip number one! Always working out with your friends limits you. I want you to try out some new partners this week."

Yasmine and Tameka were now partners, and they started laughing. Bobbie's plan hadn't worked very well with them.

But Tess *was* facing a complete stranger. She stepped forward and stuck out her hand. "Tess Adams."

"Kim Carson." The girl shook Tess's hand.

Kim was big—about two inches taller and twenty pounds heavier than Tess. Her leg muscles were well defined. She had light blond hair cut close to the scalp and intense blue eyes.

Tess paid close attention as Bobbie described a complicated passing and dribbling drill. The partners were supposed to start twenty yards apart. Then the girl with the ball was to dribble forward, make a short pass to her partner, and run backward to receive a long pass.

"I'll start," Kim announced.

"Fine." Tess would have preferred to start herself, but she didn't want to make an issue of it.

They got into position and Kim began to dribble. She ran at a full-out sprint and didn't seem to be in any danger of losing the ball.

Kim's pass rolled directly to Tess, who didn't have to move even an inch to get the ball. By the time Tess got ready to pass back, Kim had already backpedaled a good ten yards. She ran confidently, her eyes on the ball between Tess's feet.

Tess passed. Without glancing down, Kim got control of the ball, changed direction, and began dribbling back toward Tess to repeat the sequence.

Wow, Tess thought. While the girls continued to run the drill, Tess found herself wondering about Kim. Where was she from? And where had she learned to dribble as if the ball were part of her body?

Bobbie kept the fast-paced drills coming. Before long, Tess's lungs were heaving for air. Still, she was having a great time. She studied the way Kim touched the ball, moved her feet, held her eyes. Tess was used to practicing with the Stars, where she was one of the best players. Okay, probably *the* best. Working out with someone who could run circles around her was fun. Kim could teach her a lot.

"Okay, girls, time for lunch!" Bobbie called around noon. "You have two free hours. Eat, take a nap, whatever. But make sure you're rested and ready to go at two. I have a big afternoon planned for you!"

Tess spotted Tameka, Letitia, and Yasmine standing together near the halfway line. They were obviously waiting to walk back with her. She held up a finger to indicate that she'd be there in a minute. Then she approached Kim, who was wiping the sweat off her face with a little towel she'd brought.

"You were great out there," Tess said.

"Thanks."

"I was wondering if you wanted to have lunch with me and my friends," Tess said. "I thought we could—"

"No." Kim's reply was automatic. Without even saying thanks, she walked off.

Tess felt as if someone had slapped her in the face. How rude could you get?

"Yo, Adams!" Yasmine called. "If we don't get

to the mess hall soon, all the food will be gone! Are you coming, or what?"

"Coming!" Tess jogged toward her friends, still feeling stunned.

"What were you talking to Kim about?" Letitia asked as they started toward the mess hall.

"I asked her to eat lunch with us."

Letitia chuckled. "What did she say?"

"She said no." Tess shook her head, still surprised by how rude Kim had been. "And man, was she unfriendly! I mean, there's no way Kim could dislike me that much. She doesn't even *know* me."

Letitia nodded as if she'd heard it all before. "Don't take it personally," she said. "That girl is *cold*."

They reached the parade ground and headed directly toward the mess hall.

"Does she have any friends?" Tameka asked.

"A few. But none of them play well," Letitia replied. "I'd bet you a hundred dollars Kim is hanging out with a bunch of girls who barely made the Competitive section."

"Sounds like *she's* a little competitive," Yasmine said.

"She likes to *crush* her opponents," Letitia said.

"Well, she may not be nice," Tess said. "But she's got some terrific moves."

Yasmine held open the mess hall door for her friends. They went to pick up trays.

"I was watching you guys run drills," Tameka told Tess. "And I don't think Kim is much better than you."

"Thanks . . . but she is. I can't believe they didn't put her in Elite."

Letitia smiled as she reached for a bowl of chocolate pudding. "I bet she's a little shocked too. That's probably one of the reasons she's in a bad mood."

Tess could relate.

★

During free time that evening, Tameka, Tess, and Letitia hung out in the sitting room in their cabin while Yasmine took a shower. Letitia had brought a portable CD player with her, and Tameka was flipping through her CD collection.

Letitia was removing her nail polish. "Who do you think will get nominated to be captain?" she asked.

"I haven't really thought about it," Tameka admitted.

"Kim, definitely," Tess said. "She's the best player in our group."

"Yeah. But if she's as nasty as you say, who would nominate her?" Tameka asked.

"She'll talk someone into it." Letitia sighed. "I hope I don't end up on her team. That would be three days of torture."

Tess gave Letitia a look. "Who would you want to boss you around for three days?" she asked.

Letitia considered as she took out a little bottle of white nail polish and shook it. "Tameka wouldn't be bad," she said.

Tameka's head snapped up. "Me?" she squeaked.

"Sure," Letitia said. "I'd nominate you."

Tameka stared at her new friend. She was so surprised, she didn't know what to say. She hadn't considered the possibility that she might be nominated. AYSO teams like the Stars didn't have captains. Tameka wasn't even sure what one did.

Letitia giggled. "You should see your face! You look terrified. Don't worry, I won't nominate you if you don't want to do it."

"Well . . . I'm not sure," Tameka said. "What do you think, Tess?"

"I think you'd be a terrific captain," Tess said.

Tameka got a warm, fuzzy feeling. She tried— and failed—to hold back a smile. She knew that one reason she never got to stand out on the Stars was because Tess always grabbed the spotlight. For that matter, the same thing happened at school. She was happy Tess would pass up this chance to be a leader and give her a shot. Being a captain was definitely a New Tameka kind of thing to do.

"Okay, go ahead and nominate me," Tameka told Letitia.

chapter 7

"LET'S HAVE A QUICK SCRIMMAGE TO SEE how you use the skills we've been drilling," Bobbie suggested toward the end of the morning session on Monday.

The thirty-three Advanced girls were working in two groups. Letitia and Tess were in Bobbie's group. Tameka and Yasmine were working with the other coaches.

"Tess, Kim, Marcie—play attackers for the black team," Bobbie said.

Tess waited to hear what specific position the coach wanted her to play, but Bobbie moved on to the rest of the lineup.

Marcie and Kim were already over by the equipment bag, so Tess jogged over and pulled out a black singlet. "Is Bobbie going to give us actual positions?"

Marcie, a short, dark-haired girl with an easy smile, shook her head. "She never does. She thinks it's good for us to fight it out among ourselves. Is it okay with you guys if I take left wing?"

"Sure," Tess said.

"I'll play center," Kim announced. She began dribbling toward the halfway line.

Tess felt a flash of irritation. She didn't like Kim's attitude. She acted as if she were the only one good enough to play center.

Well, I'll just have to change her mind, Tess thought.

The girls lined up, and the other team—the reds—took the kickoff. Bobbie was acting as ref.

The red right wing drove the ball forward, easily outmaneuvering Marcie. But then she came face-to-face with Letitia, who was playing midfielder for the blacks.

The red wing passed inside.

Letitia easily intercepted and began to dribble the ball up the middle of the field. She saw that Tess was open and dumped the ball in her direction.

Tess caught it. She took off so fast that Kim and Marcie were eating her dust. That meant Tess had nobody to pass to—but who cared? She charged up the field with only three players in her sight: two red defenders who were closing in from either side and the red goalkeeper.

As soon as one of the defenders got too close, Tess gave the ball a powerful instep kick. The ball brushed by the defender's nose, soared into the goal area, and dropped into the net.

Bobbie clapped. "Okay, that's the way to do it. Come on, girls! Don't let Tess outrun you!"

Marcie gave Tess a businesslike pat on the back. "Nice going."

"Thanks."

Letitia fell into step with Tess as the girls headed back into position. "That was pretty, but you'd better watch out. Kim is going to be mad at you now."

"Give me a break!" Tess said.

Letitia shrugged. "Live and learn."

About eight minutes later, the black team got

back into the scoring third of the field. Kim had the ball—and three red players buzzing around her like flies.

"I'm open!" Tess hollered, dashing up the field.

Kim kept dribbling, making slow progress as she powered through the defenders. Someone less talented would definitely have lost the ball.

Tess slowed her pace in front of the goal. "I'm open!"

Kim held on to the ball. She used some tricky footwork to fake out the last defender and let loose with a powerful shot on the goal.

The goalkeeper was prepared. She waited in the center of the goal, knees slightly bent. But Kim had aimed the ball so that it passed just under the crossbar—way above the goalkeeper's head. The keeper didn't have a chance of stopping it.

"Goal—black!" Craig hollered.

Kim smirked at Tess. Then she headed back to the halfway line.

Tess trailed along after Kim. She didn't get this girl—she was acting as if they were opponents, not attackers on the same team. "You might consider passing once in a while!" Tess hollered.

Kim turned back. "Passing only makes sense if you have confidence in your teammates."

Tess stopped walking. Was Kim saying she couldn't play? That was ridiculous! She'd scored a goal too.

"Line up!" Bobbie barked.

Tess trudged back to her position, feeling her anger boiling inside. Did Kim really believe she was that bad?

While she waited for the kickoff, Tess had a thought. Maybe Kim was trying to spook her. Maybe she thought she could ruin Tess's concentration by insulting her. Yes, that had to be it.

Tess shot a glance at Kim. *Well, it's not going to work,* she thought.

★

In the afternoon Bobbie broke the girls into thirds to do a series of passing drills.

Yasmine was in Liz's group.

Tess and Tameka were in Bobbie's.

Letitia was in Craig's.

At first Yasmine was bummed not to be with any of her friends. But soon she was too busy to worry about it. For the next three hours she practiced every type of pass imaginable—short passes, long passes, forward passes, back passes, running passes.

Yasmine enjoyed herself for the first two hours. Liz discovered that Yasmine had trouble aiming with her left foot and made some suggestions to help correct the problem. Yasmine concentrated on following Liz's advice.

But during the third hour Yasmine was tired, sweaty, hungry—and sick of passing. All she could think about was going back to the cabin, taking a shower, and gobbling down an enormous dinner.

"You girls look like you're about to pass *out*," Liz announced a few minutes before five. "Why don't we call it a day?"

"Yes!" Yasmine yelled. She said goodbye to a couple of girls in her group and then looked around for her friends.

Craig's group was starting to break up too.

Yasmine jogged over to Letitia. "Ready to head back?"

Letitia's face was wet with sweat. She had a ball tucked under her arm. "Not yet. Craig wants to show me something I'm doing wrong. I'll meet you back there."

"Okay," Yasmine said. "I'll wait so that we can go to dinner together."

"Thanks."

By then Bobbie had dismissed her group. *Where are Tess and Tameka?* Yasmine wondered. She finally spotted them, walking away from her, heading across the fields. They had their arms around each other's shoulders and their heads together, as if they were discussing some secret.

Yasmine felt a flash of irritation as she started to run after them. Why hadn't they waited for her? She always waited for them.

I wonder if those two even care that I'm here, Yasmine thought. She stopped running. She decided to see how long it took them to miss her. If they got all the way back to the cabin, it would prove that she wasn't important to them.

Tess and Tameka passed the mess hall. Yasmine trudged along several yards behind them, close enough to keep them in sight without their noticing her.

As they crossed the parade ground, Tameka started to kick a rock along the path. Tess was laughing about something—maybe the fact that Tameka couldn't kick the rock straight.

With each step Yasmine felt her resentment growing. Tess and Tameka had forgotten all about her! *They're just nice to me when I'm around. Otherwise they don't even know I exist,* Yaz told herself.

By the time Tess and Tameka reached the cabin and went inside, fury had filled every cell of Yasmine's body. *I could get zapped off the planet by aliens and my so-called friends wouldn't even care!* she thought.

★

Dinner that night was vegetable lasagna. Yasmine devoured two servings before Bobbie got up from the coaches' table and turned to face the campers.

"May I have your attention, please?" Bobbie called out in her booming voice. "It's time for the team captain nominations. We're going to start with the Competitive group. Please stand if you have a nomination to make."

Yasmine worked on her salad while she watched girls stand up and make nominations. Craig wrote down each name that was called out. The list was long. The coaches were going to have to do some serious work reducing the group to three.

"Anyone else?" Bobbie called. "Okay, let's move

on to the Advanced group. Stand up if you have a nomination!"

A plump girl who was sitting over by the windows stood up. "I nominate Kim Carson."

Tess made a face at her friends.

"I told you," Letitia said. Then she stood up.

"Yes, Letitia?" Bobbie said.

"I nominate Tameka—um, Tameka, what's your last name?"

The crowd laughed. "Thomas," Tameka said.

"I nominate Tameka Thomas." Letitia sat down.

Yasmine stared at Tameka. "I didn't know Letitia was going to nominate you!"

Tameka nodded. "Yeah. We decided a couple of days ago."

"How come you didn't tell me?"

"I thought we did," Tameka said. "I mean, weren't you there while we were talking about it?"

"No, I wasn't."

"Oops. Sorry."

"No problem," Yasmine said. But in truth, she was bugged. She stared out over the room as two or three more girls nominated campers she didn't know.

The coaches will probably pick Tameka, Yasmine figured. *She's been playing great ever since we arrived.*

Yasmine wondered whose team she'd be on. The way her luck was going, it would be Kim's. And Tess and Tameka would be together. They'd get all caught up in their team and forget about her. . . .

Please don't let Tess and Tameka end up on the same team, Yasmine begged silently. Then she had an idea. A brilliant idea! A way she could be almost certain Tess and Tameka wouldn't get to be together.

Yasmine stood up.

"Yes, Yasmine?" Bobbie said.

"I nominate Tess Adams."

TAMEKA SHIFTED HER GAZE FROM TESS to Yasmine, trying to figure out what was going on. Why had Yasmine nominated Tess? Were her friends playing some sort of joke on her?

"Thanks, Yaz." Tess was still holding a fork in one hand, but she seemed to have forgotten about her food.

"No big deal." Yasmine had a funny expression on her face, Tameka thought. Her skin was flushed, and she was looking down at her plate, pretending not to know that everyone at the table was staring at her.

Letitia caught Tameka's eye and shook her

head in disbelief. "Tess, are you saying you didn't know that Yasmine was going to nominate you?"

"Nope."

Letitia turned on Yasmine. "What were you thinking? You knew Tameka was running."

"No, I didn't. Nobody told *me*."

"Nobody *had* to tell you!" Letitia argued. "You were sitting right there. You saw me stand up and you heard me nominate her."

Yasmine shrugged.

"Let's not fight," Tameka said. "This isn't a big crisis. All Tess has to do is tell Bobbie she doesn't want to run."

"Why would I do that?"

"Why not? You said you were going to sit this one out."

"I never said that!"

Tameka blinked in surprise. So she'd been wrong about Tess wanting to give her a chance to shine. She'd felt all warm and fuzzy for nothing. Great. "I—I guess I misunderstood."

Tess sat back and took a deep breath. "Listen, we're getting upset over nothing. Let's not worry about this until we find out who the coaches pick.

This isn't about you, Tameka. I never would have asked Yaz to nominate me. But I'm glad she did. I want to make sure one of us gets elected and shows Kim who's who."

"Fine," Tameka agreed. But she couldn't help feeling disappointed that Tess and Yasmine weren't being more supportive.

★

Things in Barcelona were quiet that night. When the girls got back from the evening activity, Letitia went off to hang out with some of her friends from the summer before. She didn't get back until right before lights out.

Yasmine had gotten a care package in the mail from her parents. After ripping it open, she lay on her bunk, flipping through the new *Fourteen* magazine they'd sent and munching some home-made chocolate chip cookies.

Tameka was listening to one of Letitia's CDs through headphones on her portable CD player. Tess was puttering around, cleaning up. Yasmine couldn't help noticing that Tess and Tameka were hardly speaking to each other. Apparently they both felt bruised from the big blowup at dinner.

Yasmine heard a click as Tameka pushed the Off

button on the CD player. She glanced up and saw Tameka, headphones in her hand, watching her.

"What?" Yasmine asked.

"I was just wondering." Tameka's voice was low. "Are you mad at me for some reason?"

Yasmine's heart started to beat faster. This was her opportunity to tell Tameka how left out she'd been feeling. She hesitated. *Why should I make up with Tameka now?* Yasmine asked herself. *Just when she's starting to feel miserable for a change?*

"No," Yasmine said as evenly as possible. "I'm not mad at you. Why would I be?"

Yasmine saw the computer printouts as she came out of breakfast the next morning. A crowd of girls was gathered around them.

Now we get to find out who the captains are, Yasmine thought. She almost dreaded seeing the list. Part of her was hoping that the coaches hadn't picked both Tameka and Tess to be captains. Then her friends wouldn't have any reason to fight. But another part of Yasmine was enjoying the trouble she'd caused.

"Come on," Tess said. "Let's find out who the coaches picked."

Yasmine, Tameka, Letitia, and Tess waded into the crowd. They pushed forward, angling for position. Scanning the papers, Yasmine spotted the Advanced group. The captains' names were written across the paper in bold black letters.

KIM CARSON.

TAMEKA THOMAS.

TESS ADAMS.

They picked both of them! Yasmine thought.

Tameka backed away from the list and caught Tess's eye. "Are you going to quit now?"

"No. You?"

"I—I can't."

A rush of emotions flowed through Yasmine. She felt satisfied. Uneasy about what would happen next. And guilty—after all, Tess and Tameka *were* her friends. Even if they forgot her sometimes.

Letitia let out a low moan. "What did I do to deserve this?" she muttered.

"What?" Yasmine asked.

"I'm on Kim's team."

That reminded Yasmine to check whose team she was on. She read down Kim's list first and felt a surge of relief when she didn't see her name. She checked Tameka's list next. There she was.

Yasmine wasn't thrilled with her assignment. She'd felt uncomfortable around Tameka ever since she'd nominated Tess. Oh well. At least it was better than getting stuck with Kim. And the most important thing was that Tess and Tameka weren't together.

★

"Attention, everyone!" Craig said to Tameka's team a little later that morning. The Blue Mug teams had each gathered for their first practices together. Craig's foot was resting on a cardboard box. "I want you to meet your new team captain— Tameka Thomas!"

Yasmine half expected Tameka to announce that she'd changed her mind and didn't want to be captain. Tameka liked to avoid conflict. But Tameka stepped forward and gave the group of ten girls a high-voltage smile.

"Thanks," she said. "Um, like Craig said, my name is Tameka. I play soccer on an AYSO league in Beachside, Michigan. AYSO is all about having fun, improving your skills, and making friends. I hope we can do all those things over the next few days."

Tameka looked down at the grass for a moment and then seemed to decide she had more to say.

"But I also came to Camp Aspire to prove something to myself," she continued. "I wanted to find out if I have enough, um, fire inside to be a great player. So have fun during the tournament. But, please, work hard too. Because I want to take that Blue Mug home."

"Yay!" shouted a few girls near the back. Apparently Tameka wasn't the only one who wanted to win.

"Open the box!" called a girl with dark hair. "Let's see what team we are."

"Oh—okay." Tameka kneeled down and opened the box. The rest of the team pushed forward.

"What color are the shirts?" someone demanded.

"Yellow," Tameka said.

"Yellow?" One of the girls pushed forward for a better look. "No. They're gold—all right!"

Two girls started hopping around in circles. "Tigers, Tigers! Yay!"

Even Craig was grinning.

"Are the Tigers a good team?" Yasmine asked a girl who was standing next to her.

"The best!" the girl said. "Grrrr! We can't lose now! The Tigers never lose."

★

When they got to the mess hall that afternoon, the usual small, round tables had been replaced with long ones. Each table had a different-colored tablecloth. A gold one had been set up near the salad bar.

"Are we supposed to eat with our team?" Yasmine asked one of the Tigers, a girl named Jan.

"It's not exactly a rule," Jan told her. "But it helps us think like a team. Besides, we don't want the *enemy* to see our lineups or anything."

"Oh—right," Yasmine said with a smile. She couldn't help wondering what Marina would think of the Blue Mug. All this talk about *enemies* wasn't very AYSO—but so far everyone seemed to be having fun.

Yasmine went through the line and then slid into a seat next to Tameka. "I guess we're not going to see much of Letitia and Tess for the rest of camp."

"I guess not."

"Tameka, what did you mean earlier when you said you came here to prove something?"

Tameka took a sip of her milk, looking a little embarrassed. "Remember when Marina passed out our certificates at Tosca's?"

Yasmine nodded.

"Mine said 'Best Assister.'"

Yasmine thought about that. "So?"

"It was like when Tess said she's going into Hollinsworth's class next year," Tameka said. "It made me feel like I'm second best. I used to think Tess was crazy with all her goal setting and her extra-credit projects. But maybe she had it right all along. Maybe I need to push myself hard to do something great."

"You always play well, Tameka."

"Sure," Tameka agreed. "But I'm not sure I've ever performed my best. Not at school; not at soccer. I've always done just enough to get by, or to help someone else score a goal. I'm getting curious about what might happen if I push myself."

Yasmine mulled that over. "So you want to win the Blue Mug . . ."

"Yeah! To prove to myself that I'm the best at *something*. The worst part about that Best Assister Award was that everyone seemed to agree it was a good award for me. But I think of myself as more than an assister."

"Heavy."

Tameka made a face. "I know! I keep wondering if some sort of weird hormone attack is behind all this."

Yasmine laughed. But she found herself hoping that the Tigers would win the Blue Mug. It wasn't going to be easy. They would have to beat Kim—and Tess.

chapter 9

"KIM IS THE WORST!" LETITIA announced as the girls walked home from the evening activity, a soccer trivia game. One of the
older Advanced girls had won on the question:
Which now-retired New England Revolution
player is nicknamed the Spiderman? Answer:
Walter Zenga.

"Poor Letitia." Tess was in such a great mood,
she even had sympathy to spare for Letitia. As far
as she was concerned, that day at camp had been
the best one so far.

Tess loved being captain of her own team, the
Wolves. The fact that Bobbie and the other
coaches had picked her had to be a good sign.

Olympics, here I come! Tess thought. She was wearing her gray Wolves T-shirt to show her team spirit.

Letitia was carrying her dark blue T-shirt balled up in one hand. Kim's team was the Sharks.

"That girl has such a swelled head, I'm surprised it fits through doors," Letitia said.

Tameka laughed as she walked into the cabin. "Come on. She can't be that bad."

Letitia glared at her. "She is! I *swear*. She thinks winning the tournament will be a piece of cake. At one point this afternoon Liz said, 'Don't forget you're going to be competing against two strong teams.' Know what Kim did?"

Yasmine started pulling off her shoes. "What?"

"She laughed!"

"You're joking!" Yasmine said.

"No, I'm not. She laughed right in the coach's face."

"Brave," Tameka said.

"Well, I don't think she should be so sure of herself," Yasmine said. "The Tigers look strong."

Tess saw Tameka give Yaz a little smile. "So do the Wolves," Tess added quickly.

"Kim isn't worried about the Tigers. She thinks

you guys are all too nice to play tough." Letitia slid a look at Tameka. "She called you a marshmallow."

Tameka rolled her eyes. "Who cares what Kim thinks?"

"Did she say anything about me?" Tess asked.

Letitia nodded vigorously. "Oh yeah. Get this, she said you have such a big ego, the Wolves will probably all quit—and you'll end up a lone wolf."

Yasmine and Tameka laughed at that.

Tess forced a smile, but she didn't think Kim's comment was funny. She thought back on that day's practice, scanning her memory to see if she'd said anything that might have annoyed her team. Tess hated how Kim could make her feel so unsure of herself. Especially since, for all she knew, making her uneasy was Kim's goal. She probably knew Tess and Letitia were cabinmates and guessed that Letitia would report back.

Or was she being completely paranoid?

Either way, Tess knew one good way to shut Kim up.

Beat her.

★

Tameka stared into the mirror as she brushed her teeth.

You're going to have to bring it up, she told herself firmly.

She had spent the entire evening waiting for Tess to say something about the fact that they'd ended up in direct competition with each other.

Tameka had never imagined herself in this position. But she couldn't back down now. Backing down was simply not a New Tameka kind of thing to do. Still, playing against Tess felt weird. And Tameka couldn't help wondering how Tess felt about competing against *her*.

She zipped her toothbrush back into its case, resolving to mention the subject herself. When she walked into the main room, she found Tess sitting at the table as if she had been waiting for her. Yaz and Letitia had already gone to bed.

"Meeki," Tess said. "We have to talk."

Tameka sank into a chair, feeling relieved. "I know," she said. "What do you think about all this?"

"It's simple—we have to beat her."

"Beat who?"

"Kim! We have to make sure she doesn't win. And the only way we can do that is by working together."

Tameka had no idea what Tess was talking about. But it sounded harmless enough. Especially that part about "working together."

"Sure," Tameka agreed. "So, things are okay between us?"

"Definitely," Tess said happily.

★

Late that night something woke Tess up. She stared into the silent darkness for a few seconds. Then she heard something moving in the sitting room.

As quietly as possible she dropped out of her bunk. She padded into the sitting room and saw Letitia tiptoeing toward the door.

"Where are you going?" Tess whispered.

"To have some fun with Kim." Letitia waved something that looked like a small envelope over her head.

"What is that?" Tess whispered.

"Cherry Jell-O."

"What are you going to do? Give her a sugar headache?"

"You'll see," Letitia whispered. "It's all been carefully planned. I even got her bunkmate to help me. Want to come?"

"Um, no thanks," Tess said. "But good luck."

"Suit yourself." Letitia moved toward the door.

Tess headed back to her warm bed. *Maybe Letitia's practical jokes aren't that bad,* she thought sleepily. *Especially if they're aimed at Kim.*

But what was up with the Jell-O?

★

Bobbie looked from Tess to Tameka to Kim. "Any questions?"

"I've got it," Tess said.

"Seems clear to me," Tameka added.

Tameka glanced at Kim long enough to see her nod. She had to bite back a smile. Kim's fair skin was stained with pale red streaks. She looked as if someone had tie-dyed her face, arms, and legs. Kim didn't seem to know who had pulled the stunt, so she was covering all her bases by being extra nasty to everyone.

Tameka knew Letitia had sprinkled cherry Jell-O in Kim's bed. While Kim was asleep, her sweat had melted the Jell-O, and the dye had soaked into her pores. Letitia said even showering wouldn't get the stains out right away. Kim was going to spend a few days looking like a pink-and-white zebra.

"Okay, I'll give you five minutes to explain the rules to your teams," Bobbie said. "Then we'll get started."

Tameka walked back to the Tigers and gave them an encouraging smile. The faces in the group were beginning to look familiar.

The short, dark-haired girl was Marcie. She lived in downtown Chicago and ran very fast.

Yasmine was chatting with Jan, who looked as if she should be playing basketball, not soccer. She was about seven inches taller than Yasmine. Jan was a bit clumsy when it came to running, but her skinny legs were strong, making her a great defender.

Then there was Roxy. With her bleached-blond hair and a tattoo of barbed wire on her wrist, Roxy looked tough. But she was sweet—unless you tried to sneak a ball by her when she was tending goal.

"Gather round, everyone," Tameka said. "The first event is shooting and goalkeeping. Our entire team is going to rotate through the goal. While you're in the box, one player from each of the other teams will take a shot from twenty yards out."

"So we only have to defend against two shots?" Jan asked.

"Right," Tameka said. "After we've all had a turn in the goal, we'll switch. Tess's team will take the goal while we shoot. Then Kim's team will take the goal, and we'll shoot again. The coaches will keep track of which team makes the most goals. Whoever does, wins. Any questions?"

Tameka was pleased when all her team members shook their heads. They looked focused and ready to compete.

"I'm supposed to decide what order we'll go in," Tameka told her team. "Roxy, I'd like you to go first. You're great in the goal, so you'll give us all confidence."

Roxy nodded her agreement.

"Everyone else—think about where you'll be comfortable. I think our strongest goalkeepers should go first, and the rest of us follow up."

"I want to go early and get it over with," Yasmine announced.

"Okay," Tameka agreed. She started to make notes on the clipboard Craig had lent her. She quickly worked out a lineup that made almost everyone happy. She handed it over to Bobbie, who would make sure it stayed the same for all three rounds.

A few minutes later Roxy put on the goalkeeper's gloves and moved confidently into the goal. The rest of Tameka's team waited on the sidelines.

Kim's team lined up on the left side of the field, Tess's on the right. Tameka was pleased to see that Kim and Tess had each elected to be the first member of their team to shoot.

"I guessed Tess and Kim would go first," Tameka told Yasmine. "That was the *other* reason I wanted Roxy to be first in our lineup. She's probably the only Tiger who could stop their shots."

"Very sneaky." Yasmine smiled.

And effective. Tess and Kim both failed to get the ball by Roxy. The less talented shooters who came later were matched up with less talented goalkeepers. Just as Tameka had planned.

At the end of the first round, Kim's Sharks were in the lead with four goals—one of which Letitia had made. Tess's Wolves had three.

The teams changed positions.

Tameka watched as Tess took her place in the goal and immediately started pacing. Marina had made Tess play goalkeeper during one of their games the previous season. That was the only time

Tameka could remember seeing Tess stopping balls. She loved attacking positions too much to spend much time practicing defensive ones.

Kim lofted her shot right over Tess's head and into the net.

But Roxy missed.

When Tameka's turn came up, she tucked her shot into the corner of the net. Then she went to the end of the line to watch the rest of her team shoot.

Yasmine seemed almost businesslike as she took her turn. Her shot went in, right between the goalkeeper's feet. She was grinning as she joined Tameka.

"We're good," Tameka greeted her.

"I know. I think we're going to win this event."

"Me too."

The second round ended. Tess's Wolves, who had been in the goal, still had three points. Kim's Sharks had nine. And Tameka's Tigers had six.

The teams switched positions again. Kim's team had one great goalkeeper, one so-so goalkeeper, and nine dreadful ones. Letitia was so bad that Tameka suspected she'd let both balls by her just for the fun of seeing Kim turn purple.

At the end of round three, the score was Tameka's team 14, Kim's team 9, and Tess's team 8.

"Captains, please!" Bobbie called.

Tess, Tameka, and Kim jogged over.

Bobbie was making notes on her clipboard. "Three points goes to the winning team," she said as she wrote. "That's you and the Tigers, Tameka. Two points to Kim and the Sharks for coming in second. And Tess, the Wolves get one point. Okay, now listen up while I tell you about tomorrow."

Tameka's gaze wandered to her team. The Tigers were clustered together, laughing and talking excitedly. On the camp's other fields, the Competitive and Elite girls were involved in competitions of their own.

"Tomorrow we test your dribbling skills," Bobbie was saying when Tameka tuned back in. "You guys are going to take turns pairing your players for one-on-one scrimmages."

Tess was frowning thoughtfully and squinting toward Tameka's team—probably already trying to decide which of her players would do best against which of Tameka's.

"Each pair will play for two minutes," Bobbie continued. "The object of the game is to have possession of the ball when the time-out bell rings. The team with the most possessions wins. Sound simple enough?"

"Sure," Tameka muttered. She was already planning her strategy. The way she figured it, her team would have a big advantage if she could pair each of her players with someone slightly less talented.

As soon as Bobbie dismissed them, Tameka headed toward the sidelines. She wanted to get her clipboard and make some notes on Tess's and Kim's players before they disappeared.

chapter 10

BEFORE HEADING BACK TO THEIR CABINS, Tameka and some of the Tigers made a side trip to the mess hall. Just as Tameka had hoped, the team lists were still hanging on the wall.

Tameka copied down the names of the girls on Tess's and Kim's teams. Then the Tigers did their best to remember everything they knew about the players' dribbling styles.

Slowly Tameka started to get an idea of which of her players would stack up well against the competition.

"What can we do about Kim?" Tameka wondered aloud.

"Hope someone on Tess's team gets stuck with her," Roxy suggested.

Tameka smiled. "Yeah. Well, we should have a plan just in case. How about if we match her up with Marcie? That girl can really run."

"I think Angela would be a better choice," Jan said.

"Angela?" Tameka pictured the girl. Quiet, skin and bones. "She's a good dribbler?"

"She's okay," Jan said. "But she's on Kim's team at home. I'm figuring she probably knows more than the rest of us about Kim's style. That could give her an edge."

"Good thinking!" Tameka said. By that same logic, they figured Tameka or Yasmine should take on Tess.

The girls kept at it until campers began to arrive for dinner. "Let's quit," Tameka suggested. "I don't want Tess or Kim to know about our list."

Tameka slipped the paper under the others on her clipboard.

Yasmine headed back to the cabin. But Tameka detoured to a big building known as HQ, the place they'd signed in on the first day of camp.

Bobbie, the other coaches, and the camp nurse had their offices inside. A bank of pay phones ran along the front of the building. Tameka wanted to call home and tell her family how great things were going at camp. She was punching in the number when Tess appeared at her side.

"Where have you been?" Tess asked.

"I had some Tiger team business to deal with."

"Well, I've been looking all over for you. Can that call wait? We have to talk."

Tameka hung up, surprised at Tess's tone. She sounded mad.

"Sure. What's wrong?"

"Let's go somewhere private." Tess walked swiftly toward a trail that led off into the woods.

Tameka shrugged and followed Tess up the trail. Even though it was almost six o'clock, the sky was still bright. "What's up?"

Tess stepped off the trail and perched on a large flat rock. "I want to know why you didn't let my team score more! You promised to help me beat Kim. And we came in in last place!"

Tameka stared blankly, not quite getting what Tess meant. "S-Sorry," she stammered.

"I'll forgive you—*if* you make it up to me tomorrow."

"How?"

"Let my team win."

"How can I do that?"

"Simple. Pair your least talented players with members of my team."

"But . . . I can't. My team would know something was fishy. And besides, Tess"—Tameka lowered her voice—"you're asking me to *cheat*."

Tess groaned, and her whole body went limp. "Meeki, please don't start that."

Tameka was silent. She knew that once Tess decided she wanted something, she did her best to get it. She wouldn't let a few rules get in her way.

"Listen," Tess said. "I know you couldn't care less about the Blue Mug." Her tone seemed to say no sane person *would* care. "But I feel like someone has to knock this Kim Carson off her high horse. Preferably me. So I'm asking you to help. Is that too much to expect from your best friend?"

Tameka felt like rolling her eyes. Tess was laying the guilt on pretty thick. "Tess, *this* competition *is* important to me," Tameka said quietly. "You know I've been feeling like a loser ever since Marina gave me that award—"

"Meeki!" Tess interrupted. "I can't believe you. It's not like you to be so selfish."

Tameka blinked. "You think *I'm* being selfish?"

"Totally. I mean, you're acting as if what *you* want is the only important thing."

"And what are you doing?"

"Something completely different. I don't want to win just for the glory. Or to give myself a boost. I want to show Kim Carson she isn't God's gift to soccer. It's totally different."

"I . . . guess. But, so why can't *I* beat Kim? That way everyone's happy."

Tess looked a little embarrassed. "Listen, Meeki, you're my best friend and I love you. But when it comes to playing to win, you're not exactly a . . . tiger. You're more like a pussycat. Beating Kim is too important to mess up. And I really think I'm the best person for the job."

Tameka felt miserable. Who was she trying to kid? The new Tameka was still the same old "Best Assister" Tameka. "All right, I'll do it," she said.

★

By the time the pairing was half over the next morning, Tameka felt as if her stomach were trying to digest itself. It kept churning.

Helping Tess win was not all that easy, Tameka discovered. Each time one of Tess's players came up, Tameka had to evaluate the players she had left and choose one she thought would lose. When Kim's players came up, Tameka had to choose a Tiger she thought would win.

"Tameka, who would you like to pair with Kim?" Bobbie asked.

"Um . . . Roxy."

Jan drew closer. "I thought we decided to give her Angela."

Tameka shook her head. "I changed my mind," she whispered.

Jan frowned, but she backed off.

Finally the pairing was over and the competition began.

"Tameka, Tess, why don't you two go first?" Bobbie suggested.

Tess had picked Tameka as her opponent. Tameka guessed that Tess was expecting her to lose on purpose. *Well, that* is *what you promised to do,* Tameka reminded herself.

★

Yasmine watched her friends take their positions in opposite corners of a twenty-yard box like prizefighters getting ready for a bout.

Tess and Tameka faced off against each other. It was exactly what Yasmine had wanted when she nominated Tess for captain.

But now Yasmine found it difficult to enjoy the scene. Ever since she'd found out how important the Blue Mug was to Tameka, Yasmine had been feeling guilty about what she'd done. She knew Tess wouldn't give up the competition without a fight—and that meant someone was bound to get hurt.

The only question now was: Would it be Tameka or Tess?

★

"On your mark, get set—" Bobbie blew her whistle.

More from instinct than anything else, Tameka dashed toward the ball. Tess got there first. She controlled the ball and began dribbling it around the perimeter of the square.

Tess was moving fast. Tameka, however, didn't

have a ball to slow her down. She could run at full speed. In a flash Tameka caught up to Tess. Reaching between Tess's legs from behind, she drew the ball away.

That was easy, Tameka thought. Then it hit her—it was easy because Tess hadn't expected her to play to win. She was supposed to lose.

Oops.

Tameka slowed her pace, letting Tess catch up. This time Tameka pretended to be outmaneuvered. She allowed Tess to steal the ball. The ball had only been back in Tess's possession about two seconds when Bobbie blew her whistle.

"That's one for the Wolves."

Tameka trudged back to the sidelines.

Yasmine gave her a pat on the back. "That's okay. We'll catch 'em."

Tameka forced a smile. She wished she could tell Yasmine what was going on. But Tess had made her promise not to. She'd argued that Yasmine was a Tiger. She might not like it if she knew her team captain was trying to lose.

Next one of the Wolves went up against a Shark. The Shark won. Then it was Jan against a so-so player on Kim's team. Jan won.

The score was 1 all. But as more and more girls took their turns, Tess's Wolves started to rack up the wins. Her team ended up coming in first place, followed by Kim's Sharks and then Tameka's Tigers.

The overall scores were tied at 4. That afternoon, one of the teams would be eliminated. *Too bad it has to be mine,* Tameka thought unhappily.

chapter 11

THE GIRLS WERE HEADING TO LUNCH that afternoon when Tess motioned for Tameka to let Letitia and Yasmine walk ahead.

"This afternoon is the obstacle course," Tess whispered.

"I know," Tameka whispered back. "I'm not sure I can do much to make sure my team loses."

"I've been thinking about that," Tess said. "Bobbie says each team has to select four girls to run the relay."

"Well, I can't just put in the worst girls," Tameka said stubbornly. "Everyone will know."

"I agree," Tess said. "So this is what I think you should do. Make sure you're on the Tigers. Then trip."

Tameka felt her heart sink. "Tess, I don't want to do that."

"Meeki. Don't back out now. It's too late."

★

"Okay, guys, the obstacle course is this afternoon," Tameka told the Tigers after lunch. "Only four of us can run it. So we have to pick a team."

Tameka hesitated. She didn't feel comfortable just announcing that she wanted one of the four spots. But if she was going to help Tess, she had to be on the team.

"Um, any idea how we should choose?" Tameka asked.

"I'm out," Jan said immediately. "Dribbling is not my best skill."

"Or mine," Angela said quietly.

"Or mine," Roxy added.

"Okay," Tameka said. "That takes it down to eight. We still need to eliminate four. Should we draw straws?"

"I have a better idea," Yasmine said. "Let's each add up the points we've made for the team in the events so far. The four players with the most points can do the relay."

Tameka smiled at Yaz. "That's a good plan."

Everyone agreed and began tallying up points. In the end, the Tiger team was Tameka, Yasmine, Marcie, and a girl named Keiko.

Part of Tameka was unhappy she'd made the team. Now she didn't have any excuse not to help Tess.

★

"Wow," Tameka said when she saw the obstacle course. Three lines of plastic cones marched at regular intervals down the field, dividing the playing area.

"Oh no," Marcie breathed when she saw the course. "My coach at home never has us dribble around cones. I'm not sure I'm going to be good at this."

"You'll do great," Tameka said.

Marcie shrugged uncertainly. She started shaking out her legs.

Yasmine came to stand next to Tameka. "Tess is great at this kind of stuff," she said with a frown.

"I know." Tameka felt a stab of nervousness for the Tigers and then reminded herself not to be stupid. She already knew the Tigers were going to lose—because she was going to make sure of it by falling.

"Captains!" Bobbie called.

Kim, Tess, and Tameka jogged over to the head coach.

"Okay, guys," Bobbie said. "This event is simple. When the whistle blows, one member of your team will take the ball up the field, dribbling in and out through each cone. Then she'll turn around and come back, this time dribbling around two cones at a time. When she crosses the goal line, the next member of the team will take the ball and do the same thing."

"What if someone messes up?" Tameka asked. "Skips a cone or something like that?"

"Good question," Bobbie said. "If you miss a cone, one of the coaches will blow a whistle. You have to go back and dribble around the cone correctly. Okay, you've got five minutes to warm up and then we'll start."

By the time the relay teams lined up behind the goal line, Tameka was practically shaking with anxiety. Somehow she had to run well enough that her teammates wouldn't suspect she was cheating, and badly enough so that the Wolves would win. Not exactly fun and games.

"First runners, please take your places," Bobbie said.

Kim and a Wolf Tameka didn't know stepped forward. Yaz was running first for the Tigers. Bobbie placed three balls on the goal line, and each girl positioned herself behind one.

"On your mark, get set—" Bobbie blew a piercing note on her whistle. The runners took off.

"Go, Yaz!" Tameka hollered.

Yaz and the Wolf were dribbling confidently, moving smoothly around the cones. But Kim was faster. She was ahead by almost four cones when she lost control of the ball. It bounced a few feet ahead of her in the direction of the touchline.

"Yes!" Tess shouted.

Tameka watched closely as Kim ran after the ball, drove straight back toward the course, and began dribbling through the cones again.

Bobbie tooted her whistle. "Sharks, you missed two cones."

Kim ignored her. She kept dribbling around the cones, fighting to regain her lead.

Bobbie blew her whistle again. "Kim!" she shouted. "Go back and get the cones you missed."

Kim plowed forward.

By now Kim's team was on its feet, shouting at her. "Go back! Go back!"

Kim stopped the ball. Her face was red as she turned to Bobbie. "I didn't miss any cones!" she hollered.

Bobbie shook her head in apparent disgust. She said something to Kim in a low voice. Tameka couldn't hear Bobbie's words, but they seemed to do the trick.

Kim backtracked to the spot where she'd lost control and began dribbling again.

At this point Yasmine and the Wolf were nearly finished with the course. Yasmine was slightly ahead.

Without meaning to, Tameka caught Tess's eye. Tess shot her a look that seemed to say, *Don't forget our deal.* Tameka felt a flash of irritation. Kim was losing—wasn't that enough for Tess?

Yasmine and the Wolf passed their balls off to their second runners. Tess's new runner took off at top speed. Marcie was running for the Tigers. She crawled down the course, taking each cone with exaggerated care.

Tameka looked at Yasmine and Keiko. "Well, she warned us. She really *isn't* any good at this."

Keiko shrugged. "Don't worry. We still have plenty of time to catch up."

When the second runners came in, the Tigers had fallen well behind the Wolves. The Sharks were in distant third, still making up for Kim's disastrous start.

Keiko got the ball from Marcie and sprinted off.

The Wolves' third runner was fast. But near the end of the line she missed a cone.

Bobbie tooted her whistle. "Missed cone—Wolves."

Tess's runner immediately went back to correct her mistake. But Keiko was pouring on the steam. As she headed back toward the goal line, Tameka could see that Keiko was a full second ahead of the Wolves.

"Look at Letitia go!" Yasmine said.

Tameka turned her attention to the Sharks' course. Sure enough, Letitia had regained lots of ground for Kim's team. She was only about two cones behind Keiko and the Tigers. The Sharks were back in the race.

Tameka's heart was pounding as she got ready to run. She felt someone's eyes on her and looked toward the group of Wolves. Tess was beaming her a pleading gaze. Tameka gave her a tiny nod, then looked away.

Marcie patted Tameka on the back. "It's all up to you now."

"Don't mess up," Yaz added.

"Don't worry, I won't." Tameka's eyes were on the ball. Keiko passed off to her. Tameka caught the ball and dribbled into the course. She was aware of Tess on her right, moving swiftly through the cones. Out of the corner of her left eye, she could sense a Shark nearby.

If I fall, Tameka thought, *Tess and the Shark will both pass me and the Tigers will be eliminated.*

Tameka had finished half the course. She turned the ball around and began dribbling back. Now she could see Marcie, Keiko, and Yaz jumping up and down on the goal line. They were cheering as if their lives depended on winning this race.

Do it now, Tameka ordered herself. *Fall down!*

But her feet didn't seem to be paying attention. She kept on dribbling, swiftly closing the space between herself and her cheering teammates.

Then, *swoosh!* Momentum carried her over the finish line, still on her feet.

"We won!" Marcie hollered.

Yaz threw her arms around Tameka. "Way to go, cap-*ten!*"

Tameka looked around, fighting to catch her breath. "Who came in second?"

"Um . . . the Wolves," Keiko said. "But *we* won. I am so psyched! My team has never won the Blue Mug before. Last year I was a *Bear.*"

Now the rest of the Tigers had poured out of the stands and were making their way onto the field. They surrounded the relay team, pounding them on the back. Everyone was grinning and chattering with excitement.

Tameka could easily imagine how sad they all would have been if she had tripped and they'd lost. *You did the right thing,* she reassured herself.

"Look at how horrible Kim is acting," Keiko said. The whole team turned their attention to the

Sharks. Kim was screaming at her teammates for losing—apparently forgetting that the loss was her fault.

"I can't believe Kim's team is out of the running," Marcie said.

"Just one event left—a game against the Wolves," Yasmine put in. "Then the Blue Mug is ours."

Marcie grinned. "*If* we win."

"*When* we win," Keiko said. "It's a done deal."

chapter 12

"WE HAD A DEAL," TESS WHISPERED INtensely. "And you blew it."

It was past lights out. Tess and Tameka were in bed. Tameka had a thin sheet pulled over her, and even that was making her hot. The temperature was hovering in the eighties and the night was still, without a breeze.

"I already said I'm sorry. I shouldn't have promised to cheat. I just couldn't do it."

Tess didn't answer right away.

Tameka stared at the bottom of Tess's bunk, waiting. Her leg muscles ached from the workout she'd given them over the past few days, but she felt wide-awake.

"Listen," Tess finally said. "I understand what happened today. But just because you chickened out once doesn't mean you can't help me tomorrow. Your team won't know about it. All you have to do is not score yourself. Tell Bobbie you want to concentrate on coaching, and stay on the sidelines. Or pretend to have a bad day."

Tameka imagined sitting on the sidelines, watching her team lose. How depressing! Maybe they could win without her . . . and maybe *not*. Her team only had three good attackers—and she was one of them.

Tess seemed to take her silence for agreement. She dropped her head over the side of her bunk. "Thanks a lot, Meeki. I appreciate this."

"I haven't agreed to do it yet!"

"You agreed to do it two days ago."

"I did *not*!" Tameka sat up. She glared at Tess's face in the half-light. "I only agreed to help you beat Kim. And she's out of it now."

"I know that!" Tess's voice was loud.

"Shhh! Molly will hear."

Tess's breath was coming in fast, angry bursts.

"Tess." Tameka tried to take a let's-be-reasonable

tone. "I thought you were only concerned about not losing to Kim. But that's not an issue anymore."

"That doesn't change anything."

Tameka felt her temper flare. "So you're saying you don't want to lose to *me* either?"

"Yes!" Tess hollered. "I don't care who I'm competing against. I want Bobbie to know I'm the best Advanced captain. You have to help me win."

A knock came on their door, loud enough to make Tameka jump.

"Who is it?" Tameka asked.

"Letitia."

Tameka let out all her breath at once. She got up and ran to open the door. "I thought you were Molly."

"I'm surprised she's not in here. You guys totally interrupted my beauty sleep."

"Boo-hoo." Tess dropped out of her bunk. She pushed past Letitia, out into the sitting room.

"Where are you going?" Tameka called, trying to keep her voice down.

"I don't know."

"But it's after lights out."

"So I won't turn any lights *on*."

Tameka flopped down on her bed. She put her head in her hands. "Where's Yaz?"

Letitia sat down next to her. "Asleep. I think the competition today tired her out."

"Either that, or all the dancing she did at Disco Night," Tameka said.

"Do you want to talk?" Letitia asked.

"About what?"

"Well, from the sound of it, war is about to break out in bunk one—weird behavior for best friends."

Tameka sighed. "Promise not to tell?"

"Promise."

"Tess wants me to let her win tomorrow."

"Get out of town!"

"Shhh! Molly . . . remember?"

Letitia lowered her voice. "You said no, I hope."

"Well . . . not exactly."

"How could you even think about losing on purpose? What about the Tigers? You're their *captain*."

Tameka sighed heavily. "I know. But I'm also Tess's best friend."

"If you ask me, you should find yourself a new best friend. A *real* friend. One who won't ask you to cheat. Girlfriend, don't you know when someone is *using* you?"

"Listen, I know you don't like Tess. But she's actually terrific. And I don't want to lose her friendship. In fact, I came to camp to prove I was as good an athlete as Tess, to make sure we stay friends."

"Well, you're going to have to dump Tess—or let down your team." Letitia got up and moved toward the door. "You choose."

After Letitia was gone, Tameka lay on her back. She stared up at Tess's bunk. *Which will it be?* she asked herself. *Tess or the team?*

★

"Letitia told me you and Tess had a fight last night."

"She did?" Tameka slid Yasmine a look.

Tameka and Yasmine were alone, on their way to morning practice on field four.

"Yeah. She said I should ask you what it was about. So . . . What was it about?"

Tameka hesitated for a split second. But she had to tell Yasmine the truth. They were friends. "Tess wants me to throw the game so Bobbie sees what a good captain she is."

Yasmine stopped walking. She looked as if Tameka had punched her in the stomach. "*Today's* game?"

Tameka nodded, caught off guard by her friend's reaction. She'd expected Yasmine to take the news in stride. After all, Yaz knew Tess. She shouldn't be surprised by how obsessive Tess could be about winning.

"But what about Jan and Roxy and Keiko?" Yasmine asked. "What about *me*? How could you make that decision for all of us?"

"Tess just asked me to hold back. She thought if I didn't score—"

"Well, it's the same difference! The Tigers are counting on you! Besides, didn't you tell me you came to camp to prove you were the best at something?"

"Yes."

"Did you mean cheating?"

"Don't be stupid!"

"So what are you going to do?"

"I don't know."

Yasmine rolled her eyes. "Maybe Kim was right. Maybe you are a marshmallow."

★

As the Tigers stretched out, Yasmine kept a close eye on Tameka. She'd never seen her look so troubled—and she knew she was partly to blame.

If she hadn't nominated Tess, Tameka wouldn't be in such an awful situation now.

Yasmine considered telling Tameka why she'd nominated Tess. But she decided confessing now would be selfish. From the sound of it, Tess was treating Tameka pretty badly. *Tameka doesn't need to know I'm an awful friend too,* Yasmine told herself. *At least, not yet.*

Tameka put her body on autopilot during practice that morning. She felt like a robot—running sprints, doing drills, smiling at her teammates. Meanwhile her mind was far away, trying to figure out what she should do that afternoon.

As the practice sped by, Tameka's anxiety grew. She'd have to make a decision soon.

"That's it, everybody," Craig called a few minutes before noon. "Good luck this afternoon!"

Yasmine fell into step with Tameka as the girls headed back toward the mess hall. They trudged along silently for a while.

"Think of it this way," Yasmine said just before they went inside. "What would Tess do in your shoes?"

Tameka laughed. She didn't even have to think about that one. Tess would never, ever lose a game on purpose. Tameka turned the fact over in her mind a few times and realized her choice was obvious.

"You're right," Tameka said. "I'm going to tell Tess that if she wants to win, she's going to have to beat us fair and square."

Yaz grinned. "Cool deal."

Tess's team was making a racket in the mess hall, howling like a pack of lunatic wolves. Tameka thought they were funny. But she needed to talk to Tess, and she couldn't exactly go up to her table and suggest a private chat. *Who knows what those Wolves will do if I invade their territory?* Tameka thought.

So she waited until she saw Tess get up and head for the mess hall rest room. Then she followed.

When Tess came out of the stall and saw Tameka, she smiled. "Hey! Ready for the big game this afternoon?"

"Well, almost," Tameka said, dreading what she had to say next. "But I have something important to tell you. I—I'm not going to do what you asked. I can't."

Tess's smile faded. "Can't, or won't?"

"I don't know. . . . Won't, I guess. Tess, try to

understand. Winning this game is big for me. I need it."

"Why?"

"Just to prove I can win," Tameka said. "To show I have it in me. Please try to understand."

Tess's expression grew darker. "Do what you have to do," she said coldly. "But don't expect me to say it's okay."

"Tess, come on! Be reasonable. You're asking me to do something you wouldn't do in a million years!"

Tess stared at her. "I'm asking you to do something you would have considered no big deal a few weeks ago. You never used to care about winning. Sometimes I think I don't know you anymore." With that, Tess pushed through the door and disappeared into the hallway.

Tameka leaned back against the sinks and let out a slow, shaky breath. Things definitely weren't turning out the way she'd planned. She'd come to camp to cement her friendship with Tess, not to fight with her.

Still, Tameka knew she couldn't give in to Tess now. Giving in would involve something worse than letting her best friend down—it would mean letting herself down.

Being the new Tameka wasn't easy.

chapter 13

"Five minutes!" Bobbie barked.

"Okay, gather around for the lineup," Tameka said. Her heart was beating wildly, but she tried to look calm and confident. The Tigers' game against the Wolves was about to begin.

Field one was alive with players from both teams. The Tigers were wearing their gold T-shirts. They had black-and-gold tiger stripes painted on their faces. Tess and her teammates were suited up in their gray Wolves T-shirts.

The bleachers were full. Most of the campers from the teams that had already been eliminated had come to watch the big event. Letitia was sitting with some of the Sharks. And Tameka spotted Kim sitting alone, her face set in an angry scowl.

"I'm going to play left attacker," Tameka announced. "Yaz, you're in the center—"

"Against Tess?" Yasmine squeaked.

"Well, probably. But you're not going to be facing her alone. This is a team effort." Tameka gave Yasmine a wink and then continued through the lineup. She put Roxy in the goal. Jan was a defender. Marcie was playing center midfield.

"Any questions? Suggestions? Problems?" Tameka asked.

Everyone looked happy—except for Angela. She was frowning uncertainly.

"Did you want to say something, Angela?" Tameka asked.

Angela flushed, but she nodded. "Well, I, um, you put me in the midfield. I don't think that's the best idea."

"Don't be silly," Tameka said. "You'll do a great job."

"That's not it," Angela said hesitantly. "It's my ankle. I broke it last winter and it's feeling achy today. I may not be able to run that fast."

"Oh."

"I'll switch with her," Keiko offered. She was supposed to play defender.

"Great." Tameka scribbled the changes on her lineup and turned it in to Bobbie.

Bobbie called the captains onto the field. Tess came over. She stood waiting for the coin toss without even saying hello to Tameka.

Tameka shifted her weight nervously, hoping she had made the right decision. Playing to win wouldn't mean much if Tess never spoke to her again.

The Tigers got the kickoff.

Craig, who was acting as referee, put the ball down on the halfway line. "Let's get started!" he called.

Yasmine and Austin, the Tigers' right attacker, joined Tameka on the field. They got into position.

So did the Wolves. Tess was playing center attacker.

About a minute into the game, Austin sent Tameka a pass. Tameka controlled the ball and took off up the left side of the field. She gained a few yards before Tess began pursuing her.

Tess stuck to Tameka like a burr, batting continuously at the ball.

I've got to pass, Tameka thought. She glanced right. But Tess was shielding her from the rest of the field. Tameka couldn't see Austin or Yaz. But she did get a quick glimpse of Tess's face. Her expression was so intense, so angry, that it almost frightened Tameka.

While Tameka was looking at her friend, she stumbled on something. A rock, maybe—she couldn't tell. She staggered sideways, fighting to regain her balance.

Tess saw her opening. She tried to kick the ball free of Tameka's feet. But she hit it too hard. The ball bounced out of bounds.

"Throw-in—Tigers!" Craig called.

Tameka stepped over the touchline, scooped up the ball, and took a second to read the field. Tess was covering Keiko, who was playing left midfielder. Most of the other Tigers were covered too. Only Yaz was open. Unfortunately, she was standing way off in the middle of the field.

Just get it to her, Tameka told herself. She threw the ball over her head with more power than she'd realized she had. The throw was a bit short, but close enough.

Yasmine moved sideways to collect the ball. Then she quickly turned and drove it forward. She slammed the ball into the net before Tess's defense had time to react.

"Way to go, Yaz!" Tameka called.

"Nice one!" Roxy hollered.

Tess's face flushed an angry red.

Craig placed the ball. Seconds later one of the Wolves passed to Tess, who whizzed past Tameka and tried to drive into Tiger territory.

Tameka hovered near the halfway line, staying in position and nervously watching Tess dribble closer to the Tigers' goal. Tess managed to get off a powerful shot. But Roxy was there. She rolled the ball out to Angela, who booted it back to the halfway line.

The Tigers mounted another attempt on the Wolves' goal, getting close enough for Yasmine to shoot. But her aim was off. The Wolves got a goal kick. They were still trying to get into scoring position when Craig blew his whistle.

"That's the half! Take ten."

"Nice half, everyone!" Tameka told her teammates. "Just remember, we haven't won this game yet."

Tameka could see Tess pacing along the opposite sideline. She wasn't resting or chatting with her teammates. She just kept moving, glaring down at the grass in front of her. Even from across the field, Tameka could feel her friend's determination.

She knew she didn't look half as fierce as Tess. But that didn't mean she was going to give up.

★

Two minutes into the second half, Tess drove the ball into Tameka's territory. Her right attacker ran along only a few yards away.

The two girls tapped the ball back and forth, moving fast and passing so frequently that Tameka's defense was caught off guard.

Tess shot.

"Get it, Roxy!" Tameka yelled.

The ball jumped at Roxy, heading straight toward her face. Roxy tucked and put her hands up to catch the ball. It glanced off her hands and rolled slowly into the net.

"Goal—Wolves!" Craig hollered.

Yasmine looked up at the sky and sighed. "This isn't good."

Tameka patted her on the back. "Don't give up. We still have almost twenty minutes to score."

Austin overhead. "It might help if we could get the ball."

Tameka understood how her teammates felt. For most of the second half, Tess had been dominating the game. But the Tigers were still in it.

"We can win," Tameka told the others. "All we need is one more goal."

About three minutes remained in the game when Tess sent a scorching shot toward the bottom left corner of the Tigers' goal.

Roxy was standing on the opposite end of the goal area. She took two hopping steps and then dived. Her arms were outstretched, fingers grasping. She landed on her belly. Tameka could see Roxy's chin snap back as it hit the ground.

Tameka closed her eyes. Even from her spot back by the halfway line, the fall looked painful. It also looked as if Tess's shot was going to go in. If it did, that would be the end of the Blue Mug. The Wolves would win.

Tameka opened her eyes and saw Roxy struggling to her feet, the ball clutched tightly to her chest. She drop-kicked it away from the goal. The Wolves hadn't scored!

"Thank you, Roxy!" Tameka yelled.

The ball arced high over the field, and Tameka could tell it was going to land near the halfway mark.

"Let's go!" Tameka yelled.

Yasmine and Austin took off at top speed. Tameka ran with her eyes on the ball, trying to judge where it would come down. The ball hit near the halfway line and bounced.

Marcie jumped up, trapping the ball with her right foot. She got control and passed forward. "Coming at you, Captain!" she shouted.

Tameka ran after the ball, heading up the center of the field. She caught it and sent it skittering in Austin's direction.

Austin drove forward maybe a foot, then passed the ball back to Tameka.

Tameka was close to the goal, a little off to the side. She had about half a second to decide what to do.

Pass to Yaz? No, she was too far away. One of the Wolf defenders would intercept.

Pass to Austin? No, she was covered.

Pass back? Maybe—but that would waste time, and they didn't have much of that.

Suddenly Tameka realized she had another option. She could shoot herself. The shot was tricky, but not impossible. She pulled her foot back and kicked the ball in so hard, it rolled under the net and kept going.

"Goal—Tigers!" Craig hollered. He paused for a beat. "And that's the game!" he added.

Tameka sank onto her knees, laughing with relief and happiness. It was over. She had won.

AFTER THE GAME THE TIGERS AND Wolves lined up to shake hands. Tess moved down the line, murmuring, "Good game, good game," over and over. Actually, she thought the game had stunk. She'd lost—and there wasn't much chance Bobbie would be impressed by *that*.

She could see Tameka down at the end of the line. As Tess got closer, she started to feel panicky. She couldn't face Tameka. Not yet. Maybe not ever.

Tess had an image in her mind. She kept seeing Tameka sink onto her knees at the end of the game, laughing with happiness. Seeing that made Tess feel ashamed of herself.

Tameka tried to tell me how important this game

133

was to her, Tess told herself. *But I was determined to win at all costs.*

As the line moved forward, Tess ducked her head and slipped away.

★

Dinner at the Tigers' table that evening was fun, Yasmine thought. The team kept breaking into rowdy chants of "Ti-gers, Ti-gers, Ti-gers" while pounding on the table.

Roxy refused to speak. She growled instead.

But Yasmine's attention kept wandering up the table to where Tameka sat picking at her food. She didn't exactly look happy.

Yasmine picked up her plate. She asked Keiko to move so that she could sit next to Tameka.

"Hi." Tameka gave Yasmine a weak smile as she slid into the seat.

"How are you doing?" Yasmine asked.

Tameka shrugged. She was carefully lining her peas up in a row.

"You should be celebrating," Yasmine said softly. "We won, you know."

Tameka made a face. She ran her fork through the peas, scattering them. Then she started lining them up again. "I guess I'm not in the mood."

"Where's Tess?"

"I don't know." Big frown. "I haven't seen her since after the game."

Yasmine felt a prick of worry. Tess *had* lost the Blue Mug, and her best friend *was* mad at her. She probably wasn't feeling that hot right about now. "Maybe I should go look for her," she suggested.

"Whatever."

Yasmine took her tray up to the kitchen and headed back to the cabin. She looked for Tess in her room, but it was empty. So was the bathroom. Finally Yasmine found Tess—lying in Yasmine's own bed. She looked grim.

"Hi," Yasmine said.

"Hi."

"We were getting worried about you. Aren't you going to eat dinner?"

"I'm not hungry."

Yasmine felt uneasy. She'd known Tess for years, but she'd never seen her so bummed out. It was as if someone had drained all the life out of her. "Well, the last campfire is beginning soon," she said. "We're going to make s'mores. That should be fun."

"I guess. Yaz, will you do me a favor?"

"Sure."

"Switch rooms with me tonight. I don't want to have to share with Tameka."

"How can you be mad at her?"

"I'm not mad at her—but I'm sure she's mad at me. Do you mind switching?"

"No."

"Thanks."

There didn't seem to be anything more to say, so Yasmine headed back outside.

She walked slowly down the path toward the parade ground. *You got exactly what you wanted,* she told herself. *The way things are going, Tess and Tameka will probably never be friends again.*

So why did she feel so miserable?

Well, part of it probably had to do with the fact that Tess and Tameka were about the last two people in the world she felt like hanging out with now. They were both acting like big mopey drags. She hated seeing her friends so unhappy.

Yasmine walked back into the mess hall, where the party was still going strong. She sat next to Letitia.

"Where have you been?" Letitia asked.

"Checking up on Tess and Tameka."

"How are they?" Roxy asked.

"Not that good."

Letitia shrugged. "If you ask me, Tameka is better off without Tess. I'm glad they're fighting."

Yasmine smiled. "Oh yeah? Well, guess who wants me to switch beds with her tonight?"

"Not Tess!"

Yasmine nodded.

Letitia shuddered. "I think it's time those two made up." A smile slowly formed on her face. "And I know just how we can get them together."

Tameka was talking to Jan when Letitia ran up to their table. "I'm so glad I found you!" Letitia said. "Yaz and I have been looking for you all over. Come on. Hurry! She's waiting."

"Who's waiting?"

"Bobbie. She's in our cabin, and she said she needed to talk to you right away."

"What about?"

"She wouldn't say."

Tameka gave Letitia a doubtful smile. "Is this one of your practical jokes?"

"Hey, if that's what you want to believe . . ." Letitia's tone made it clear that she didn't care one way or the other. "But if I were you, I wouldn't keep the head coach waiting."

"You'd better go, Tameka," Jan said. "Maybe she wants to give you a prize or something."

That didn't sound very likely to Tameka. But she got up and followed Letitia outside. Something felt fishy, but she didn't see any harm in making sure Bobbie *wasn't* waiting for her.

Tameka walked into Letitia and Yasmine's room. Bobbie wasn't there—no big surprise. But Tameka *was* surprised to see Tess lying on Yasmine's bed, reading.

The second Tameka entered the room, Tess looked up from her book and stared.

Tameka suddenly realized what Letitia was up to. She was trying to get her together with Tess. Yaz had probably put her up to it. *Well, it's not going to work,* Tameka thought. She turned to flee. She caught a glimpse of Yaz and Letitia in the sitting room—and then the door slammed in her face.

Tess saw the door slam from her perch on the top bunk. She felt as if her blood had turned to ice. She didn't want to be locked up with Tameka, and she was sure Tameka didn't want to be anywhere near *her*.

"Did they lock us in?" Tess asked.

"Yes."

Tess dropped out of the bunk. She crossed to the door and gave it a yank. The door wouldn't budge. "Let me out!" she yelled.

"No way!" Yasmine shouted from outside. "You're locked in, and you're both staying there until you make up."

"Great," Tess muttered.

Tameka shrugged and sat down on Letitia's bunk.

Tess slid her back down the wall until she was sitting on the floor. "I hope they don't mind being out there all night," she murmured.

Tameka's head snapped up, her face distorted with anger. "Why?" she shouted. "Is it going to take you that long to forgive me for something *you* did wrong?"

Tess blinked. She wasn't used to Tameka losing her temper, and she had no idea how to react. Tameka's behavior had been all over the place since school ended. Sometimes Tess felt as if she were watching Tameka morph into a whole new personality.

"A lot of people around here think *you're* the one who should be sorry. Not me!" Tameka's voice was quieter now, but she still looked furious. "You were totally out of line asking me to cheat. And all that stuff about having to beat Kim was bull. You just wanted to win! And you know I'm a good enough player to beat you."

"Well . . . yeah."

Tess saw a series of emotions pass over Tameka's face. First the anger faded, and she looked surprised. She almost smiled. Finally her forehead wrinkled and she looked confused. "What do you mean—yeah?"

"I mean . . . I agree."

"Go on."

Tess sighed. "Well, I shouldn't have asked you to cheat. I guess I had a hard time thinking of you as being on another team. I mean, I'm used to having you on *my* team. Plus, you were a great captain. Your team really liked you and played their best for you. It wasn't like that on my team."

Tameka sat up and crossed her arms in front of her chest. She didn't look impressed. "Hmmm . . .

Well, even if we had been on the same team, it's not right to cheat."

"I know. But I had to choose between losing and cheating. Cheating seemed like more fun."

"Why do you hate losing so much?" Tameka crawled to the end of the bed so that she could see Tess's face.

"I don't know."

"It's not like your mother would disown you if you lost."

"I know."

"And your friends wouldn't hate you or anything."

"I know. But losing makes *me* miserable."

"Are you miserable now?"

"Well, yeah." Tess laughed a little. "But I feel better now that we're talking again."

Tameka laughed. "Me too."

"So can we still be friends—even though I have strange psychological issues about always being the best?"

Tameka pretended to consider. "Why not? I mean, who else would want your twisted little soul?"

Tess got up and gave Tameka a hug. "Thanks."

"No prob."

"Tess, do you really think I was a good captain?"

"Meeki, you were the best. Even better than me!"

Tess crossed to the door and knocked on it. "Okay, you can let us out now!"

"Not until you make up!"

"We did make up!"

"Prove it!"

Tess and Tameka exchanged exasperated looks. "If you just open the door, you'll see our happy, shining faces!"

chapter 15

YASMINE OPENED THE DOOR A CRACK and stuck her head in. "Let me see."

Tess and Tameka stuck their faces in front of the crack and gave her big goofy smiles.

Yasmine laughed. She opened the door all the way, bounced into the room, and plopped down on Letitia's bed. "That was fast. And I hardly heard any yelling and screaming."

Tess tried to look disappointed. "Yeah, it wasn't much of a fight. No blood, no loose teeth."

Tameka laughed. "You didn't even yell *once*."

"Yeah, but *you* did! I almost passed out from shock and amazement."

Yasmine was thinking that if Tess and Tameka

wanted a bigger fight, she could certainly provide one. She could tell her friends how rotten they'd made her feel by ignoring her. That would make them feel good and guilty. They'd probably tell her they were sorry and swear never to do it again. They might even cry a little.

Oh, what's the point? Yasmine asked herself. She already knew Tess and Tameka were her friends. She didn't need them to tell her.

Tameka let out an enormous sigh. "You know, I still don't understand how we got into this mess. Yaz, how did Tess convince you to nominate her for captain?"

"I didn't!" Tess protested.

Yasmine felt her stomach knot. It looked as if the truth was about to come out. "Nominating her was my own idea," she admitted quietly.

"Why?"

"I wanted to make sure the two of you didn't end up on the same team."

"Why?"

"I was mad at you guys."

"What for?"

Tess and Tameka didn't look angry. At least,

not very. Their expressions were more . . . perplexed.

"I don't know," Yasmine began miserably. "Because you guys made me sit in the front seat on the way here. And you went to the Sports Shack without me. . . ."

Yasmine let her voice trail off. Now that she had spoken her grievances out loud, they sounded stupid.

But Tameka was nodding sympathetically. "You felt left out."

"Well, yeah. Big-time, actually."

"I understand," Tameka said. "I felt jealous ever since you and Tess decided to go to camp together."

This was news to Yasmine. "You did?"

"Big-time."

"Well, I haven't exactly loved having the two of you on the Tigers without me," Tess put in. "Especially with all that stupid growling you were always doing!"

Yasmine felt a smile breaking over her face. "I guess that with a group of three friends, including everyone all the time is tough."

Tameka nodded. "I'm sorry your feelings were hurt."

"Me too," Tess added.

"I forgive you," Yasmine said. But there was something else she wanted to bring up. "I call the backseat for the way home!"

★

The bonfire began just after dark. Tameka sat with the Tigers, Letitia, and Tess. They ate s'mores until they felt sick. Molly led the group in a round of the Camp Aspire song.

Then Bobbie stepped up in front of the fire where everyone could see her. She put a cardboard box she was carrying down at her feet and held her hands up for silence. The crowd quickly quieted.

Bobbie started by thanking all the coaches and campers for a great week, and then she got down to the exciting part.

"At Camp Aspire, we award the Blue Mug to the winning tournament teams." Bobbie held up one of the mugs, which was ugly in the extreme—blue plastic with CAMP ASPIRE stamped in white. "These mugs are a symbol not only of these girls' talents, but also of their captains' leadership abilities."

Bobbie paused and adjusted her glasses. "In the Competitive group, the Blue Mug goes to Alicia Peterson and the Eagles!"

Alicia stood up and took a little bow. Her team cheered as she walked up to Bobbie and collected her team's mugs. She came back to the table doing a little cha-cha dance.

"In the Advanced group, the Blue Mug goes to Tameka Thomas and the Tigers."

Tameka stood up, doing her best to look cool and relaxed. Her heart was thumping painfully. And when her teammates started to cheer and growl like tigers, she felt a smile creep onto her face. As she walked toward Bobbie, she heard Yasmine let out a loud whistle.

"Way to go, Meeki!"

That had to be Tess. Only Tess called her Meeki.

Tameka took the mugs from Bobbie and then decided she wanted to say something. She held the mugs in the air and faced the crowd.

"Thank you, Tigers!" Tameka said. "Everyone on the team helped me make decisions that helped us win! We earned these beautiful mugs with a lot of sweat and hard work!"

A roar erupted from the crowd of Tigers. "Ti-gers! Ti-gers! Ti-gers!"

But Tameka wasn't quite finished. "I also want to thank Yasmine Madrigal and Tess Adams, my two best friends in the whole world. I couldn't have done it without you guys!"

★

My two best friends, Yasmine repeated to herself. She felt her face flush with happiness.

A moment later Tameka rejoined the Tigers, and the whole team gathered around to check out their mugs.

Roxy tossed hers from hand to hand. "This is the most beautiful hunk of plastic I've ever seen," she joked.

"Hey, nice speech," Jan added. "It sounded just like the Academy Awards!"

Austin struck a pose. "I want to thank my daddy, my mommy, and my little dog, Puddles!"

Yasmine waited until things quieted down a little. Then she went up to Tameka and gave her a big hug.

"Group hug!" Tess ran over and joined in.

Tameka giggled. "What was that for?"

"Nothing," Yasmine said. "I'm just happy we're all together."

Soccer Tips from AYSO

INSTEP KICK

There are times in every soccer game when you need to clear the ball away from the front of your goal, make a long pass to a teammate, or take a really hard shot on goal. In these situations, you might want to consider using an instep kick. Though not as accurate as a push pass, it's extremely powerful.

How to perform an instep kick:

1. Decide which leg to kick with.
   You should be able to kick equally well with either leg, but you can only use one at a time!
2. Prepare the leg that will support the weight of your body.
   Bend the knee slightly.
   Place the support foot 3 to 4 inches from the ball, pointing toward your target.
   Place all your weight on that leg.
3. Prepare the kicking leg.
   Pull the leg back at the hip.
   Bend the knee and draw your calf up to your thigh.
   Position the knee so that it hovers over the ball.
4. Kick.

Keep your eye on the ball.

Whip your thigh forward.

Strike the ball at the center of your shoelaces.

Carry your leg straight through, toward the target. Don't stop the kick once you make contact with the ball.

Practice Drills:

SHOOT FOR GOAL

Put five soccer balls on the ground 15 yards in front of the goal. Using an instep kick, see how many times you can score out of the five shots you take. After you can make five in a row, have a friend play goalkeeper for a greater challenge.

INSTEP PASSING

You need a friend to practice passing. Have your friend stand about 20 yards from you. With the soccer ball at your feet, make an instep pass to your friend. Work for accuracy. Your friend will return the pass to you the same way. As you feel more comfortable with the instep pass, increase the distance between you. Once you're good at kicking from a stationary position, start passing to your friend while she's running.

AYSO Soccer Definitions

Attacker: The player in control of the ball, attempting to score a goal. Attackers need speed, power, good ball control, and accurate aim. Sometimes referred to as forward.

AYSO: American Youth Soccer Organization, a nationwide organization guided by five principles:

1. Everyone plays
2. Balanced teams
3. Open registration
4. Positive coaching
5. Good sportsmanship

Cleats: Projections on the soles of soccer shoes that provide support and a good grip on the soccer field.

Defender: The player whose primary duty is to prevent the opposing team from getting a good shot at the goal. Defenders need sufficient speed to cover opposing players, good tackling skills, and determination to win control of the ball.

Dribbling: Moving the ball along the ground by a series of short taps with one or both feet.

Goal: Scored when the entire ball crosses the line between the goalposts and underneath the crossbar. One goal equals one point.

Goalkeeper: The last line of defense. The goalkeeper is the only player who can use her hands during play within the penalty area.

Halfway line: A line that marks the middle of the field.

Halftime: A five- to ten-minute break in the middle of a game.

Midfielder: The player who supports the attack on the goal with accurate passes and hustles to get back to help the defense. Positioned in the middle of the field, she must have stamina for continuous running.

Open: A player who is not being marked or covered by a member of the opposing team is open.

Passing: Kicking the ball to a teammate.

Referee: An official who ensures the safety of all the players by enforcing the rules during a game.

Save: The prevention of an attempted goal, usually by the goalkeeper.

Scrimmage: A practice game.

Short-sided: A short-sided game is played with fewer than eleven players per team.

Substitution break: A quick break during which the coaches can put in new players and the players can grab a sip of water. Substitution breaks come a quarter and three quarters of the way through a game.

Throw-in: When the ball crosses the touchline, it is thrown back onto the field by a member of the team that did not touch the ball last. The thrower must keep both feet on or behind the touchline and throw the ball over her head.

Touchlines: Out-of-bounds lines that run along the long edges of the field.

Trapping: Gaining control of the ball by using feet, thighs, or chest.